THE S

Nonda Chatterjee has been a teacher since 1967 and is currently Principal, Cambridge School, Kolkata. She is passionate about music and gardening. This is her first book.

The Strawberry Patch

STORIES

NONDA CHATTERJEE

PENGUIN BOOKS

PENGUIN BOOKS
Published by the Penguin Group
Penguin Books India Pvt Ltd, 11 Community Centre, Panchsheel Park,
New Delhi 110 017, India
Penguin Group (USA) Inc., 375 Hudson Street, New York, New York
10014, USA
Penguin Group (Canada), 10 Alcorn Avenue, Toronto, Ontario, Canada
M4V 3B2 (a division of Pearson Penguin Canada Inc.)
Penguin Books Ltd, 80 Strand, London WC2R 0RL, England
Penguin, Ireland, 25 St Stephen's Green, Dublin 2, Ireland (a division
of Penguin Books Ltd)
Penguin Group (Australia), 250 Camberwell Road, Camberwell, Victoria
3124, Australia (a division of Pearson Australia Group Pty Ltd)
Penguin Group (NZ), cnr Airborne and Rosedale Road, Albany, Auckland
1310, New Zealand (a division of Pearson New Zealand Ltd)
Penguin Group (South Africa) (Pty) Ltd, 24 Sturdee Avenue, Rosebank,
Johannesburg 2196, South Africa

Penguin Books Ltd, Registered Offices: 80 Strand, London WC2R 0RL,
England

First published by Penguin Books India 2004

Copyright © Nonda Chatterjee 2004

10 9 8 7 6 5 4 3 2 1

Typeset in Sabon by S.R. Enterprises, New Delhi
Printed at Thomson Press, New Delhi

For my parents,
who taught me to see

Contents

Acknowledgements

I wish to thank many people, who in many ways have helped me write this book: my sister Manjari who gave me the courage to take up a pen in the first place; my husband Devkumar for giving me space and providing constant encouragement; my daughter Rupa for her faith in me; my student and friend Ayesha for devoting time and energy in typing the original manuscript and providing good ideas and constructive criticism; the men in the family, Arun, Sarvajit, Omer and Gourango for taking me seriously; my nieces Malini and Mallika for their analytical appraisal; my grandchildren—Avik, Damini, Shaheen and Aparupa—for liking my stories, and the eldest, Ananya, who said 'of course you can write a book between work and cooking'; my student Bihani, who gave me the idea of approaching Penguin; and my editors Karthika and Poulomi for their patience, time and support.

But most of all I would like to thank my younger daughter Choi for taking out time from her incredibly busy schedule to edit the book, to liaise with my editors, to write the Afterword, in which she sees my work more clearly than I do, in short, for making this book possible.

Author's Note

Her gender is the birthmark on every woman's forehead, and it dominates and influences the course of her actions, interactions, relationships, goals, struggles, failures and achievements throughout her life. This is something that my own life has taught me at some cost.

I have been fortunate to live through a period which has seen some of the most dramatic events in history: the Second World War, the country's independence and its partition, the vagaries of politics and society in post-independence India, the Cold War, the beginning of the new millennium, the wars in Afghanistan and Iraq . . . I have come to realize that the changing face of Indian womanhood in this period, perceived at a purely personal level, has been no less dramatic. The Indian woman has battled the patriarchal society, struggled for her motherland, sought release from the straitjacket of custom, defended her girl children against fearful odds, fought the narrow parochialism of religion, and transcended the petty and personal to reach for the universal.

The accounts in this book are not so much 'stories' as they are 'chronicles' based on real-life people and events spanning almost an entire century. In this collection I have tried to illumine the lives of certain 'unsung heroines' whom I have known intimately, or known of. They are a mixed bunch, ranging from figures of national importance to humble women who work as 'domestic help', are often the only earning members of their families and, on occasion, can rise to sublime heights of gallantry.

If my readers feel that I have been able to capture even slightly their incredible heroism in these pages, my labour will have been well spent.

1903

White Bulls

THE LAZY AFTERNOON SUN FLOODED THE TERRACE OF THE HUGE mansion, separated from the Ganga by a belt of lush greenery. The smooth lawns were interspersed with clumps of fruit trees—mango, jackfruit, black jamun and guava—and the tall coconut and betel nut trees along the periphery held up their graceful foliage against the sky. Behind the mansion and a little to the right lay a banana plantation and beyond that, at a safe distance, loomed the keya grove, a beloved haunt of snakes. In summer, the keya came into bloom, and thousands of flowers, odd-shaped, like banana flowers, suddenly appeared on the huge bushes with their sharp, swordlike leaves. The fragrance of these flowers was intoxicating and supposedly lured the snakes from their hideouts. When the flowers matured, the servants of the house ventured into the grove with sticks, daggers and baskets: sticks to drive away the snakes, daggers to sever the flowers from their stalks, and baskets to collect them in. These baskets with their precious burden were brought to the terrace, and the flowers laid out to dry on mats. At the right moment, always dictated by the matriarch, Chandi Debi, their pollen was shaken into huge, polished brass vessels and allowed to dry some more. When the pollen was completely dehydrated, it was sieved through the finest muslin and collected on silver thalis. Then the refined powder was poured with silver ladles into silver canisters, to be stored as a year's supply of face powder for the ladies of the house—the redoubtable Chandi Debi, wife of Sir Surendra Nath Banerjea (or 'Sir Surrender-Not' as the British preferred to call him), and her five beautiful daughters, with complexions as pale as the inside of a conch-shell, and faces so perfect that the fourth-born was affectionately called 'Patkumari', picture perfect, by her father.

The ritual has just been completed for the current year, and now the terrace is covered with oiled mats on which is spread thick, sugared mango pulp (under snow-white muslin weighed down with bricks to keep crows and impurities away). Once dry, the pulp will be cut into pieces and soaked in khir to be eaten as a delicious after-dinner dessert. Maids take turns to guard the precious sweets, thus frustrating thirteen-year-old Saraju's plan to quietly steal a piece.

Situated on the banks of the Ganga, Barrackpore, where the present story is to unfold, was of strategic military importance to the British—a base for several infantry divisions and a well-stocked arsenal. The Indian soldiers had become increasingly restive since Mangal Pandey had initiated the movement that had culminated in the First War of Independence. Mangal had managed to wound Sergeant Major Hewson and the Adjutant, Lieutenant Bogg, quite seriously before he was captured on 29 March 1857. He was court-martialled on 6 April and executed on 8 April at 5.30 a.m. The 'Sepoy Mutiny' had begun two months later when the fuse that had been lit by Pandey ignited the conflagration in Oudh, Delhi and Bihar. Indian soldiers in Barrackpore were deprived of their weapons immediately, but that did not prevent them from participating in this great war. Now, at the turn of the century, with rumours of the partition of Bengal in the air, the atmosphere in Barrackpore was tense; more so because, to Curzon's proud statement, 'The partition of Bengal is a settled fact', Banerjea had haughtily replied, 'We shall unsettle the settled.'

Though young, Saraju was surprisingly well educated for the times, for she made better use of the tutor than her brother Shankar did. She was well aware that her father's name was on the police's list of suspects and made a conscious effort to keep her eyes and ears on the alert at all times for any hint of trouble.

On this placid afternoon, however, she had no premonition of immediate danger as she swung gently to and fro on the swing on the terrace, with a book of Tagore's poems in her hands. This was her favourite haunt, and the late afternoon her favourite time of the day. She leaned back in her seat enjoying the gentle breeze and the lazy cooing of the ubiquitous but invisible cuckoo, while the lines of the poem she had just finished reading ran through her mind, 'The beautiful woman dusted her face with the white pollen of the keya . . .'

Suddenly her eyes fell on the path that led from the Ganga through the garden to the house. She saw a man running, rather awkwardly, with a group of villagers following close on his heels. Saraju closed the book with a snap and hurried downstairs.

In the hall, Chandi Debi was standing with a stricken face as the man, who had spent his last ounce of strength running to the house, collapsed, bleeding profusely from the head. The panting crowd was gesticulating wildly, all speaking at once. Slowly, the story was pieced together: some village girls had gone for their afternoon dip in the Ganga at a ghat especially reserved for them by Chandi Debi. They were returning with their pots of water when a couple of Tommies had accosted them, made indecent advances, and threatened to carry two among them off to their camp. At this point, Kalu, the wounded man, had intervened. The soldiers hit him with a baton, severely injuring him. Then other men from the village had turned up, and the Tommies had gone off threatening to return in force in a few days. Now the matter lay with the zamindarni, Chandi Debi—should the girls stop visiting the ghat and bathe in the village ponds instead?

Chandi Debi was the local landlady: the vast property belonged to her and most of the farmers paid her rent. She was a benign presence in the village, deeply involved with the lives of the village folk. When she rode down the village paths in her phaeton, one or two of her daughters in attendance, people lined the path. She stopped frequently to make inquiries, sort out small differences, or to offer help. Once a week she held court in the hall of her mansion and settled property disputes, keeping the intervention of the British magistrate to a minimum. A handsome woman, almost always clad in white, her head covered with her pallu, gold glinting on her wrists and throat, she fitted perfectly the appellation given to her by her affectionate subjects—'Ranima'. Fiercely proud of being the mother of five daughters and a woman of great moral courage she was a source of inspiration to her husband, though she could frequently be a cause of embarrassment with her strict principles and frank speech. Once, at a raja's darbar, she had brusquely refused a gift of gold bangles she had been given as the 'special guest' saying that she had enough jewellery and that the raja should make better use of his wealth. Then, when a courtesan made her musical entrance, she had walked out of the assembly. She later told her husband that she would never accompany him to such functions again.

Today, there was no doubt in her mind as to the course of action she would take. She gave her verdict: the girls must visit the ghat unafraid. Her trusted guards, the lathials who had sworn to protect her person and her land with their staves and clubs, would be posted there for their protection.

For a few days all went well. But just as Chandi Debi was about to withdraw her men, the storm broke. Seven or eight Tommies, armed with pistols, tried to abduct two women in broad daylight from the ghat. The lathials ignored the blazing guns and went for the soldiers with their clubs. Two of them lost their lives, but the others managed to beat back the soldiers and save the girls from dishonour. The soldiers, however, recognized the men as members of the rani's personal force, and swore vengeance on her and her people.

Chandi Debi was well aware that she was in a rather precarious position. Her husband was a thorn in the side of the British Raj, three of her daughters were yet to be married and her son was too young to be of help. There was no doubt in her mind that if the Tommies managed to invade the house there would be no security of life or limb and the British magistrate would turn a blind eye to the whole affair. It did not occur to her to ask for help, either from her husband, who spent most of his time in Calcutta, or her relations and neighbours. Nor did she lose her way pursuing non-essentials. As far as she was concerned, the issue was simple: the Tommies must not enter the house, and therefore their approach to the house would have to be rendered so difficult as to be near impossible.

She called to her presence the steward of her vast estate, Mahesh, and the head of the lathials, Shambhu, and placed the problem before them. After some exchange of ideas, she laid out the plan of action. As the two men listened, their smiles grew wider till Shambhu broke into loud guffaws.

'Excellent plan! No one but you could have thought of it, Ranima.'

Saraju, quiet as a mouse behind the curtain, was the only other member of the family who had any idea of the plan, and she had her doubts about it. Would such a simple ploy work against the mighty Tommies?

The day after was a busy one. The entire household, now joined by most of the village folk, men and women, was caught up in ceaseless activity. Makeshift ladders were stood up against the outer walls, allowing men to climb up and down, again and again. Saraju did her bit with quiet efficiency and bit back her words even as her siblings launched into animated discussions about what exactly the preparations were for. But still she was not quite sure. It was too simple a stratagem. Surely, her father should have been informed?

That night large quantities of strong tea with plenty of milk and sugar were brewed in huge metal containers in the kitchen and large baskets were piled high with crisp puffed rice. There was a cordon of men around the house, but the major gathering was on the roof. All night the women carried tea and puffed rice to the men, who regaled each other with stories and jokes.

'It's like the night of Lakshmi puja,' said one man. 'Usually we stay awake to ensure that the goddess of wealth doesn't leave our homes; but tonight we're keeping awake to welcome the most unLakshmi-like visitor!'

'Don't say that. After all they are the Emperor's ambassadors, the rajdoots!' replied another.

Amidst the laughter, someone sombrely interjected, 'No. Tonight is dedicated to Kali. It is moonless and dark, and we're waiting to sacrifice buffaloes to the deity. Only, these bulls are white, not black.'

Suddenly, there was a hush. The laughter and small talk died away, as the men took stock of the perilous situation.

Just as Chandi Debi had predicted, in the small hours of the morning when the men were dropping off to sleep after the night-long vigil, a contingent of twenty strong men came up the path, guns in hand, confident of executing their vengeance and escaping before the village awoke. They crouched low as they approached the house, taking advantage of the shadows of the trees and bushes.

The first flurry of projectiles, brickbats and stones took them by surprise, but still they advanced, amused at this amateurish attempt at defence. But when the flurry turned into a fusillade and three men fell unconscious, bleeding and injured, the Tommies began to panic. The enemy was invisible, but the hail of stones was continuous and only too tangible. Would even a single white man be left standing when they reached the house and broke down the solid teak doors?

Two more men fell and then another three, bringing the total to eight. By the time the harsh truth of the British adage 'discretion is the better part of valour' hit them and they stopped for a moment, two more men had keeled over. The remaining ten ran as one man at top speed back to where they had come from with cries of 'coward' ringing in their ears. Their only aim now was to sneak back into camp and into their beds, so that they could deny all involvement in this humiliating affair. They managed to creep in unobserved just as the other men in the barracks were beginning to stir.

The Commandant, shaved and bathed, resplendent in uniform and stripes, had just finished his first cup of tea before going to the parade ground, when two soldiers, fear writ large on their faces, came panting up to him.

'Please, Major, come at once. This is very serious.'

A courageous man prone to quick action, the Commandant wasted no time in following them. Just outside the barrack walls a bizarre sight met his eyes. Ten Tommies, bleeding, bedraggled and unconscious, lay stretched on the ground. A piece of cloth was pinned to the breast of one of the men. On it, in crude letters, was written, 'This is how Indians punish the dogs who dare to insult their women.' Horrified at the implications of the message, he instituted an immediate inquiry and got to the bottom of the business. Realizing that the incident showed up English soldiery in the worst possible light and that the incendiary quality of the affair could have terrible repercussions if it became public knowledge, he had the men court-martialled and shipped back to England at the earliest opportunity.

A few days later, a huge bouquet of roses arrived at the mansion. It was from the army headquarters, with the Commandant's compliments for 'Lady Surendra Nath Banerjea'. In appreciation of the peace offering, Chandi Debi sent a massive tray of sweets for the Major's family.

Sir Surendra Nath himself got to hear of the incident many months later when Saraju told him about it, after having extracted a promise from him that he would make no mention of it to her mother!

1924

The Rose Garden

A CERTAIN HOUSE IN A PROSPEROUS LOCALITY IN DHAKA IS CALLED 'Gulab Bagh', not because of the roses that grow in its sprawling garden, but because the ten daughters of Shri Ashwini Kumar Mukherjee reside there, each more beautiful than the other.

Ashwini's wife, Kailashkamini, is the daughter of a zamindar with a mindset to match. As far as she is concerned, a woman has a very specific role to play: she is to run the house, guard the wealth of her forefathers, keep her husband happy in bed and produce sons. She is deeply ashamed of the fact that she has produced ten daughters and only two sons. In an effort to make up for the numbers, she has so indulged the two boys that their future ruin is evident to anybody who meets them even for the shortest time. The many talents of her daughters have of course gone unrecognized.

Under her influence her husband, in spite of being a brilliant scholar (he is a professor of English in a college in Dhaka), has remained strictly eighteenth century in his social outlook. Though fond of his daughters, who have tremendous affection for him and wait on him hand and foot, Ashwini has had no qualms in marrying them off to largely unworthy men in poor circumstances. Chini—eight years old, as sweet as her name, with a mass of curly hair and a bewitching smile—is to be married next, and he is seriously considering getting it over and done with before she attains puberty. The reasoning behind Ashwini's decision is impeccable: he wants to earn a place for himself in heaven, and he has to propitiate a wealthy neighbour who has a thirty-year-old son, married once and widowed, now on the lookout for a second wife. Chini had caught the gentleman's eye one morning when she had run out to give alms to a beggar. He lost no time in placing the proposal before Ashwini and even offered to bear all the wedding expenses. This clinched the deal.

Before the year is out, in the month of Agrahayan, Chini is married. Fortunately, her mother-in-law is a kindly woman who delights in dressing her up in beautiful clothes and jewellery to show her off. She also ensures that Chini sleeps with her till she attains puberty. Chini, who knows no better, is happy, and comes visiting often with stories of her in-laws' wealth and affection. She also says that her husband, though a 'buro', an old man, is kind to her and had once taken her to watch a film. And so, childhood melts into womanhood and youth with its dreams remains unknown.

But this is pathos; hardly any better than the tragedy that some of the older sisters have experienced. The fifth sister, Shona, lives up to her name in looks and intelligence. Her golden skin, delicate features and curly

brown hair are complemented by her razor-sharp brain
and amazing memory. At the age of thirteen she passes
the matriculation examination in the first division, having
persuaded her brother's tutor to help her secretly with
her preparations. When her father learns of this, he
reprimands the tutor for neglecting his son and decides
immediately that Shona should be married off before
anything else goes amiss. Although there are at least three
or four scions from respectable homes in Dhaka
hankering for the alliance, Ashwini declares that being a
kulin Brahmin with an unadulterated bloodline he will
not give his daughter to any man who is genealogically less
exalted. The truth is he will not brook a son-in-law who
will rival him in any way. He is quick to settle on a young
man in faraway Khulna who is humble enough in the worldly
sense but has a horoscope that indicates his high birth.
(He also has no parents, so the dowry will be negligible.)

Thus, one summer evening, Shona comes face to face
with Dhiren under an awning in her father's courtyard.
Garland in hand, she stares into the eyes of the stranger
standing opposite her. He is as dark as she is fair, but he
is tall and well built, has a strong face and a hint of
laughter in his eyes that lights up his whole demeanour.
In that moment, Shona falls in love and decides that she
will go through the thick and thin of life with him by her
side. The next day, she boards the train with him and
goes away to a far-off village to embark on married life.

They get off the train and jolt along on a bullock cart for several miles till they come to a small river, which they cross by ferry. Then they walk the last two miles and reach a thatched cottage. 'Welcome to your new home,' says Dhiren, his kind eyes lighting up as he looks down at Shona's pretty face. A distant aunt of Dhiren's comes bustling forward to welcome the new bride. Shona, footsore and hungry, stands in a thali containing milk and alta while conch-shells are blown, and the aunt touches a woven basket, which holds a lamp and other items of good luck, to Shona's forehead, breasts and pelvic area to ensure fertility. She is made to sit on a mat while hundreds of people put sugar in her mouth and honey in her ears, so that she will hear and speak only 'sweet' words. Then she washes her husband's feet and dries them with her hair. Finally, the rites complete, she is told to bathe and refresh herself. Bathe ... where? In the pond, of course! There is one just behind the cottage that is used by the women of the neighbourhood.

Slowly, the town-bred and educated Shona learns to bathe in a pond, wash her own clothes and cook on a mud oven. She even learns how to mix mud and cow dung to make a paste and smoothen it over the floor and walls of the cottage.

Dhiren is a graduate and a schoolmaster in the village school, earning about forty rupees a month. Shona quickly learns to make a little go a long way and there is no want in their home. In the evenings, when Dhiren returns from work, they sit side by side in front of the cottage talking in whispers in the moonlight and think that life has no greater bliss to offer. Sometimes Shona brings out her esraj, a musical instrument that she plays with great joy and feeling and, when Dhiren accompanies the melodious tunes with his golden voice, the neighbours creep out of their cottages and sit around them, listening entranced.

The village girls flock to Shona's cottage when Dhiren is away at work. She teaches some to sing, some to sew, some to read. Since she does not accept payment, their cottage is filled with produce of all sorts—fruits, vegetables, fish and eggs. With the little money that they save, Dhiren buys books for his own edification and to satisfy Shona's insatiable thirst for knowledge.

Two years pass, and Dhiren and Shona are blessed with a lovely, healthy baby girl. When Dhiren gets an offer to teach in a school in a nearby town at a higher salary, Shona asks him to turn it down. The village boys need him more, she explains. But the truth is that the village with its clear streams, rippling paddy fields and lush greenery has her in complete thrall.

Then, disaster strikes, as it most often does, without any warning. A cholera epidemic sweeping the province finds its way to their remote village. Shona watches helplessly as Dhiren works day and night among his afflicted students and contracts the disease. As his life ebbs away, the spectre of widowhood, dreaded by every woman in Bengal, particularly women in Brahmin households, rises before her eyes—shaved head, white borderless sari, bare throat and wrists, one meal a day (that too vegetarian) and, most frightening of all, her little girl at the mercy of every male family member for she has no father to protect her. In desperation, Shona feeds some of Dhiren's infected faeces to their daughter and swallows some herself.

Fifteen days later, the emaciated mother and daughter turn up at Ashwini's doorstep. The mild form of the disease they contracted hasn't killed them. Kailashkamini, resplendent in a red-bordered sari and gold jewellery, personally ensures that Shona is reduced to total widowhood. Not even a single gold bangle is allowed. What will the neighbours think? Her eldest son is about to be married. What will his prospective in-laws say? The only person who protests is Moni, Shona's elder sister: 'From this day, I will wear no colour but white, even though my husband is alive. I too will eat once a day till Shona stands on her own feet.'

And so, with Moni's help and in spite of her parents, Shona goes on to educate herself, to learn English and get a job as a receptionist at the Indian Institute of Technology, Kharagpur. As she earns respect for her efficiency at her job, her confidence and her will to live re-emerge. She builds her own house, adopts a boy and ensures that her daughter gets a well-rounded education so she too may stand on her own feet if life deals her an unfortunate hand. Turning a deaf ear to her children's protestations, she performs her own shradh ceremony before she passes away because she wants to die beholden to no one.

And then there's Rani, seventh among the sisters, the loveliest, the most vulnerable and the most innocent.

In 1924, Rani is ten years old. Her father says she reminds him of 'a lotus flower on a bamboo stick', a very apt, if unromantic, description. Their old servant, Naren—Narenda to the girls—says that she is the living image of the goddess Durga, as he chases away the local boys who hang about the house for a glimpse of her. Rani herself is totally oblivious of all these goings-on and is still quite happy with her dolls, pots and pans. Unlike some of her sisters, she is not too fond of reading but plays the sitar and has a natural flair for dance.

Every year, on their father's birthday, the sisters put up a show. This particular year an unexpected visitor arrives at the Mukherjee residence on the morning of Ashwini's birthday—Mataji Tripurananda Tirtha, Ashwini's sister who had become a sanyasin when she was thirteen. Clad in saffron from head to toe, a long, red tilak on her broad forehead, and a shiny, shaved head, she is a commanding figure. Even Kailashkamini speaks in a subdued voice in the presence of her sister-in-law.

Mataji is the guest of honour at the evening's entertainment, and the few eminent neighbours who have been invited are delighted to meet her. After an opening song, Kirankumari, Ashwini's third daughter, recites Nazrul's *Vidrohi*. Kirankumari is married, has four sons and has come to visit her parents on the occasion. Tall and willowy, with rich black hair cascading to her knees, an olive skin and a face like a Ravi Varma painting, she delivers the long poem faultlessly and with all the passion that the poet had infused into it. At the end, there is scarcely an eye that is dry.

The next item is a dance-drama adapted from Tagore's *Abhisaar*. Fanny, named after Austen's heroine by her father and a year younger than Rani, plays the part of the Buddhist monk, Upagupta, for she is tall. Rani is to play the sensuous courtesan, Vasavdatta.

The scene opens in the dead of night, with the sanyasi sleeping on the roadside near the city walls of Mathura. It is a dark night, the stars obscured by thick monsoon clouds. Every door in the city is shut as people sleep soundly in their homes. And Vasavdatta, like the flame of a lamp protected by a brilliant blue veil, is on her way to meet her lover.

Suddenly, her foot with its tinkling bells

Finds itself on a human chest —
Appalled, the dancer holds up her lamp.
Its harsh rays dazzle a pair of eyes
Full of compassion . . .

In one cataclysmic moment, Vasavdatta's world is turned upside down. She bends over him and pleads:

'This harsh ground is not fit for you, young man;
Will you not do me the honour
Of gracing my home with your presence?'
The sanyasi thanks her courteously and says:
'Please go your appointed way tonight;
When the time comes,
I shall arrive at your chamber, unbidden.'

A year goes by and the scene changes: the city of Mathura is gripped by a smallpox epidemic. Vasavdatta contracts the dreaded disease. Terrified citizens carry her fever-ridden body beyond the city walls and leave her to die under a tree.

Another dark night falls. The roads are deserted as the citizens cower in their homes. A lone figure strides briskly down the streets. Tonight, Upagupta has a tryst with destiny. He steps out of the gates and finds his way to the tree under which Vasavdatta lies inert, her once golden body blackened with the pox, her throat parched with thirst. The sanyasi seats himself on the ground and lays her head on his lap. He pours water down her throat, and covers her body with a cool layer of sandalwood paste.

It is a night for love. The moon shines in all its splendour, the mango blossoms send forth their fragrance and the cuckoo sings its heart out.

> The woman stirs,
> Raises her eyes to the compassionate face,
> And asks, 'Who are you, ministering
> To me in my hour of need?'
> The sanyasi replies,
> 'I have kept my promise
> It is trysting time tonight Vasavdatta,
> I have come to you, unbidden.'

The spell lingers ... the audience is completely enthralled. Then Mataji rises and pulls her nieces to her bosom.

Later in the evening, when the household is asleep, Mataji begs Ashwini to give Rani to her. She says that if such beauty and grace do not find a place in a king's chamber, she will be fated to a beggar's hovel. No middle path is possible. She sees only tragedy in store for Rani. Why not let her become a sanyasin and give her the peace she deserves? She is certain that happiness in the conventional sense is not Rani's portion in life. Ashwini, greatly troubled, promises to think about it. When Mataji leaves ten days later, she reminds him again of her offer.

But Kailashkamini, jealous of her sister-in-law's influence over her husband, will have none of it. 'She is envious of my good luck because she is a widow,' she proclaims. 'I will certainly not allow you to throw my daughter away.'

Two years go by. Rani is twelve years old and marriage proposals are pouring in for her. Raibahadur Kumudini Banerjee, a wealthy zamindar, wants an alliance for his nephew Santosh who has just joined the Indian Civil Service. Moni, always looking out for her sisters, reminds her father of Mataji's prophecy and says, 'Surely this is an offer you cannot refuse. Baba, please say yes!' But the Banerjees are not kulins. Also, their eminence will completely overshadow Ashwini. So, although the Raibahadur is prepared to accept Rani 'in a sari, a pair of conch-shell bangles and sindur', the alliance is turned down.

Then, a proposal comes from faraway Balurghat in Dinajpur, which meets with Ashwini's approval—the man is from an eminent family, very well educated, not rich but comfortably off. They boast an unbroken Brahmin bloodline of seven generations standing. The Chatterjees, hailing originally from Illa, a village in Barishal, are greater kulins than Ashwini himself! The only snag is that the alliance is for their third son, Sudhir, whose health has been impaired by a childhood attack of pneumonia. He is a graduate and has a bachelor's degree in law, but is thin and frail beyond belief. Kailashkamini, in her infinite wisdom, passes the final judgement: 'A woman's life is ruled by her fate. If Rani is lucky, her husband's health will improve and she will find happiness.'

Rani's mother-in-law, Pramadasundari Chatterjee, however, is a very different person. Not only does she run her large household with great skill and sensitivity, but she is one of the leaders of the district Congress party and in the forefront of the nationalist movement. She is against this marriage from the start for she is well aware of her son's physical weakness, but pressure from the family is great. She tells Ashwini that they will bear the cost of the wedding, but he will have to give two thousand rupees in cash as dowry. Ashwini feels he is getting a good deal and agrees immediately.

On a chilly evening in February 1926, Rani is married to Sudhir, more than twice her age and almost a skeleton in appearance. Neighbours who have long bemoaned Ashwini's callous treatment of his daughters, feel he has outdone himself on this occasion. A relative actually walks out of the function with his family, saying that he cannot be part of such sinful proceedings. Sudhir's father, Gopal Chatterjee, opens a box full of gold jewellery and says that they have been bought with the two thousand rupees given by Ashwini so that Rani will have something to fall back on in the future. Most people feel this is a bad omen, a pronouncement of doom.

For Rani, however, living with the Chatterjees is a revelation. Unlike Kailashkamini, who had maintained her position by bullying and oppressing the rest of the family, Pramadasundari inspires universal respect and women have a place of honour in her household. She has seen to it that her own daughters are well educated, and she encourages her daughters-in-law to improve themselves in every way. Whether it is formal learning, embroidery, painting, singing, playing musical instruments, cooking or nursing, she arranges for tutors and training, and encourages them to achieve excellence. When Rani bears her first son at the age of fifteen, she tells her that of all the responsibilities she will have to shoulder through her life, bringing up her son to be a good, accomplished human being is perhaps the most important.

Pramada also works closely with the Santhals, the local inhabitants of Dinajpur. These people work on the lands of the local landlords, either as adhiars (tenant farmers who give half the produce to the landlord) or as agricultural labourers. Their women do all the household work in local homes and earn one meal a day and some money. Used to working tirelessly in the fields, household work is child's play for these women. From Pramada they learn to keep their clothes snow-white and make their brass and bronze utensils shine like gold. She has also taught them how to use locally available plants and herbs to cure minor ailments, make their hair long and dark and ease the pain of childbirth. When there is a difficult birth, Pramada moves the midwife aside and delivers the baby herself. Gradually, Rani begins to assist Pramada in whatever way she can and becomes a favourite among the Santhal women who affectionately call her 'bou'.

When the Santhals celebrate their spring festival, Basanta, Pramada's entire family is invited to the village to participate. This is the time when the mahua fruit ripens and the Santhals ferment its pulp to produce a potent punch which is distributed among all with abandon. Then, out comes the madol and men in white dhotis and women in colourful saris and heavy silver jewellery dance to its beat, round and round, faster and faster. Clapping her hands to the beat of the madol, her feet tapping restlessly, Rani can hardly restrain herself from joining the circle of dancers. And as she averts her eyes from the scene and looks around for something to distract her, her eyes fall on a young man laughing gaily at a group of children, little figures of ebony with the brightest eyes, who are dancing to their own rhythm in complete defiance of the rhythm of the madol. She has met him several times before. Saroj, the young man, is a childhood friend of Sudhir's and a frequent visitor to the Chatterjee residence. He is also Pramada's right-hand man in all her endeavours with the Santhals as well as the Congress party. About six foot tall with a square, pugnacious jaw and strong features, his brows are usually knotted in a frown of concentration. But now, as Rani watches him clap to keep the children's unique beat, a smile of utter delight lighting up his features, he looks like a different man. He turns suddenly and as their eyes meet she thinks she sees a hint of admiration creeping into his.

Sudhir's marriage to Rani has been a mystery to Saroj from the time he has been introduced to her. He has seen her a couple of times from his study window putting the washing on the roof or leaning on the balustrade and has wondered what the future holds for her, for, contrary to Kailashkamini's prediction, Sudhir's health has not improved.

By 1930 Rani has become the mother of two boys and a girl and the family expenses have increased rapidly. Sudhir's four brothers are doing well, but they resent the fact that they have to look after his family and they remind Rani of it almost every day, commenting on her three children, how much they eat, that even the clothes they wear are provided by their uncles, and so on. Realizing that things will only get worse, Sudhir moves to Dinajpur, where he gets a job as a clerk in the civil court, and Rani has fifty rupees a month to run the household. Touched by Rani's predicament, their landlady refuses to accept rent for the cottage they occupy and sends fruits and vegetables from her garden so Rani won't have to buy food.

But even with all the help they receive, Sudhir finds it difficult to stand on his own feet. His attendance at the court drops and so does his salary. Rani sends away her eldest son to her parents in Dhaka, but the younger children require medical attention which they cannot afford. Finally, an attack of typhoid confines Sudhir to bed and before family members from both sides reach Dinajpur, Sudhir breathes his last. His son, aged six, performs the last rites.

Pramada is now a widow herself and dependent on her sons. They refuse to take responsibility for Rani and her children and as much as Pramada might try, she cannot get them to change their minds. Thus, very grudgingly, Ashwini asks Rani to return to his home with her children.

Contrary to all their expectations Rani and her children find that living at home is perhaps more difficult than all the poverty they have had to endure before. Rani's elder brother, who does not have a steady income of his own, lives on his father's bounty and greatly resents this uncalled-for burden. He particularly resents Devkumar, Rani's eldest son, a quick-witted and high-spirited boy, perhaps because he himself has five daughters. He misses no opportunity to embarrass the boy and the torture he inflicts is refined and diabolically cruel.

One day, Rani finds Devkumar sitting near an open sewer with his plate of food before him. When she asks him what he is up to, he tells her in between defiant sobs that his uncle has made him sit here with his food so he knows what it is like to be dependent on somebody else for everything. For a moment Rani cannot believe her ears. Listening to her son's sobs as she holds him close, she realizes she has no words to comfort him with. Tears well up in her eyes and it takes her a while to realize that these are not tears of hurt or self-pity, but of anger; the anger she feels towards herself more than anybody else. She has always been the timid one in the family, afraid to be on her own, letting others decide the course her life will take. But now her life is inextricably bound to her children, and she cannot, will not, let anybody hurt them in any way, ever again.

Kailashkamini, still the imperious soul, and her elder son are shocked at Rani's declaration over dinner that she has decided to leave the house and live on her own with her children. Help is immediately at hand, however, for her younger brother tells her that he will give her fifty rupees a month till Devkumar begins to earn, and Chini comes to her aid and offers her a room in her father-in-law's house for a monthly rent of three rupees.

Slowly Rani discovers that she can manage quite well on her own, that there is a special joy and satisfaction in taking her own decisions. She learns that the inclusion of potato peelings makes a potato go a longer way and that pounded turmeric eaten with salt and rice is perfectly palatable. Moreover, she can save quite a bit of money this way and, within a month of living on her own, she takes the decision to shift her sons from the pathshala to St Gregory's, run by Jesuit priests. Here, under the excellent supervision of the Fathers, Devkumar excels in his studies and passes his matriculation examinations with flying colours.

The years fly by. It is now 1947. The country is paying the price for independence and the spectre of partition looms menacingly over it. On 15 September of that year, Rani leaves for Dhaka with her three children and a neighbour and his paralysed wife. They board a steamer to Gwalando and then take a train to Sealdah in Calcutta. Two days later they find themselves at the doorstep of Moni's two-room flat where she lives with her husband, three children and the two boys she has adopted.

The reunion is a happy one. The sisters are immensely happy to be with each other once again. Moni speaks often of Saroj, who has become a prominent figure in political circles after independence and has shifted to Calcutta, but still visits the Santal villages almost every weekend to see what more he can do for them. He frequently visits Moni and asks about Rani, Moni informs her with a sly smile. Rani ignores her sister's mischievous looks but is nevertheless reminded of the happy times she spent with her Santhal friends and of Saroj's kind eyes.

On Rani's insistence, Moni soon finds her a house and Rani sets up home once again. One evening, there's a knock on the door. Rani, busy in the kitchen, asks her younger son to see who it is. The voice that floats in from the next room causes Rani's heart to skip a beat. She steps out of the kitchen to find Saroj settling down in a chair.

That evening, over a cup of tea and a plate of biscuits Saroj makes Rani an offer that makes her head reel. He has always admired her from a distance and now he is in a position to offer her help, both emotional and financial. Will Rani accept his hand in marriage?

At first Rani is too stunned to respond to him. Then she refuses him, saying that it is unthinkable. If she accepts his help, people will put the worst interpretation on it, and she cannot even imagine the innumerable questions and the barrage of insidious innuendoes her children will have to face. Besides, what will the children say? How will she ever get her daughter married? Saroj tries to calm her down and make her see reason, but she will have none of it.

After he leaves, she sinks into a chair, takes a deep breath and closes her eyes. Questions rage in her mind— does she not have a right to happiness and companionship? Is there no end to this hand-to-mouth existence? But she must think of the children and their future too.

When she opens her eyes she finds her children gathered around her. They have heard everything and have something to say . . .

And so, on 31 July 1949, Rani, the most timid of her sisters, takes a momentous step, with the blessings of her children, her sisters, and amazingly even her mother and brothers. Her future life is no bed of roses, but she will never know again the grim poverty she has battled all her life.

The story of Rani's life, and those of her sisters, have been for me a personal anchor, a yardstick against which I would forever measure my own ability to surmount whatever odds life brought my way.

1942

The Strawberry Patch

A TALL GATE WITH AN ARCH OF CASCADING BOUGAINVILLEA LEADS through to an immaculately manicured lawn, a stretch of vibrant green interrupted by parterres of winter flowers bordered with conical bricks painted red with surkhi. Patches of bright sunlight steal their way between the shimmering leaves of a tall gulmohar, a graceful casuarina and a spreading peepal and dapple the neat neelkanta hedges along the borders and an arbour draped with clematis.

The house facing this garden is, naturally, colonial. It has a wide veranda, tall columns, green shutters for the tall doors and windows, and a sloping, gabled roof with protruding chimneys. Behind the house is a vegetable garden where the local sem bean jostles for space with creepers of French beans. Celery, cauliflower, beetroot, carrot, scarlet tomato, table radish, glossy purple aubergines on thorny stalks, cabbage and lush green peppers grow in neat rows around a formal herbarium replete with parsley, dill, thyme, mint, aniseed and green coriander. But the pride of this Eden—and of the lady of the house—is the strawberry patch, its runners trained over a lattice of bamboo, through which a few red berries peep out enticingly. Strawberries grow only in the hilly areas in India, and it is a measure of Mrs Mukerji's gardening skills (and her neighbour Mrs

Tucker's sound advice) that these shy plants have borne fruit in the plains. The other neighbours envy this horticultural miracle, just as they do the owners of this piece of perfection.

Mr and Mrs Mukerji, KK and Boruna to their friends, had been educated at London University and Oxford and were the epitome of the anglicized Indian. Although KK's father was the Chief Justice of the Allahabad High Court, the second Indian to earn the distinction, and KK had scored an unprecedented 200 marks out of 200 in the Civil Service viva voce examinations, he was denied a place in the elite service because one of his cousins had been interned as a terrorist and another was still in hiding. Also, young KK, in spite of his polished veneer, had not struck the right note of subservience at the interview. Finally, he had been placed as a Class I officer in the Indian Railways, where it was hoped he would not be too much of a nuisance.

This was how the Mukerjis came to live in Muradabad, a small cantonment town with a flourishing, indigenous brassware industry, the district administrative seat and the divisional headquarters of the East Indian Railway. A successful company, it had been taken over, along with others, by the British government as it was the largest moneyspinner in India, and its employees enjoyed the perks of palatial houses, a large retinue of servants, free travel and personalized saloons complete with kitchen and bar. The top positions in the railways were occupied exclusively by the British. The non-covenanted positions went almost routinely to Anglo-Indians and the domiciled English. Of late, a few 'educated' Indians had invaded this stronghold, but found it a gritty experience for two reasons: their bosses who took life really easy resented efficiency, and the ambience they were expected to adapt to was uncompromisingly post-Edwardian, with its tennis parties, balls, chamber concerts, picnics and witty social tittle-tattle.

Muradabad was strategically placed within striking distance of Meerut, Lucknow, Delhi and Allahabad, important towns and cities of the United Provinces, forerunner of today's Uttar Pradesh but much larger owing to the inclusion of Haryana and Delhi. As was the pattern, the Civil Lines with its paved roads, bungalows in large, sprawling compounds and parks was home to the British and a few 'brown sahibs'. Not too far away was the cantonment with its barracks and officers' quarters. On the outskirts of this mini-England lay the dirty, unhygienic 'native' area. The local inhabitants made their living from the exquisite brassware they produced, their work as land labourers and service to the sahibs in the capacities of cooks, masalchis (assistant chefs), bearers, grooms, gardeners and orderlies. The women worked as domestic hands and mainly as ayahs, looking after children in the British quarter till they left for boarding school in England.

Boruna was an extraordinarily beautiful young woman, her ivory skin set off by her raven hair, naturally kohl-dark eyes and arching eyebrows. Her delicate nose, her father had told her, was like Renee's, delicately *retrousse*; her mouth was sensuous and her firm chin had a deep cleft right in the centre. A young artist, madly and hopelessly in love with her, had once written in a letter that she had a perfectly proportionate face, like Cleopatra's, and that her throat was like a Grecian column. Immaculately turned out in pastel chiffons, pearls and high heels, wherever Boruna went, she made heads turn. Boruna herself was amazingly unconscious of her physical attributes and had been seriously hurt when Dr Shyama Prasad Mukherjee, Vice Chancellor of the Calcutta University, had told her father to withdraw her from the master's classes in English as she was the only woman there and the source of tremendous distraction. She had gone on to study French instead and was fluent in the language. She had also spent a term surveying Oxford prior to joining Somerville College. It was in England that she met KK and decided that he was the man she would marry. Breaking the hearts of several aspirants and suitors in Calcutta, who predictably passed many snide remarks, she had married him after returning from England.

Her erudite and loving father-in-law, with whom she struck an instant rapport introduced her to the mysteries of the Bhagavad Gita and the *Mahabharata*. With her brothers-and sisters-in-law, who found her rather westernized but utterly lovable, she had a warm relationship. But it was her approach to her mother-in-law, Lady Nalini Mukerji, that amazed everyone in the family. The lady in question—merely five feet tall, but a towering personality nonetheless—had attended the Delhi darbar when the knighthood had been conferred upon her distinguished husband. She had refused food and water at the banquet afterwards on the grounds that the food had been prepared by non-Brahmins!

In her twenty-four-room residence, she maintained her own 'Hindu department', complete with a retinue of servants of the right caste, while her husband managed the intricacies of British social protocol with the help of Muslim and Christian cooks, bearers and valets. She visited his part of the house once a day, sat with him for fifteen minutes by the clock and went back, the servants holding aside curtains and drapes so that she may not, accidentally, be polluted by them. Her only love was a black cat, Kelo, with eyes like emeralds, who spent most of his day sitting in state on a chair specially allocated to him and scratched everyone in sight except his mistress.

It took Boruna exactly a week to size up the situation. She noticed that while Nalini enjoyed intimidating people, she also held those she could bully in contempt. KK, for one, could get away with blue murder owing to his great love for her, his sense of humour and his irreverence for material things. Boruna concluded that the old lady was pining for love but was too proud to make it known. So she made up her mind, quite simply, to love the holy terror, and, as a first step, she made friends with Kelo. Bribing him secretly with saucers of milk, she soon won his confidence and appeared one day in Nalini's room with the cat draped over one shoulder, rather like a sable stole. As she asked Boruna to enter her room, a smile struggled with the usual frown on Nalini's face, but there was also a hint of jealousy at Kelo's shameless show of affection.

'So, you've captured Kelo's heart?' she asked.

'Yes, and I mean to capture yours too!'

Surprise, outrage, bewilderment, amusement and pleasure flashed across Nalini's face and, suddenly, tears streamed down her cheeks. Boruna knelt at her feet and gently stroked them, face carefully averted, until Nalini regained her composure.

'My little daughter, who left me when she was eleven years old was just like you. Not as beautiful, but the same spirit ... she was afraid of nobody, not even me.'

Boruna got up, held the old lady close for a few minutes and promised that she would not be afraid of her, but would love her till the end of her days.

In Muradabad Boruna was in complete charge of the household and the social aspect of their lives. She had realized soon enough that KK's career depended, to an extent, on how they were perceived as a couple by the families of his British colleagues and superiors. Most Indian women blindly aped their British counterparts and came off second best. Boruna played the game differently. Her drawing room, for instance, did not sport the usual chintz curtains and second-rate prints by Italian, British and Dutch masters. Rather, the drapes were beige raw silk, exquisitely embroidered in red, green and black by Boruna herself. Paintings by masters of the Bengal and Lucknow schools—Nandalal Bose, Lalit Sen, Bireswar Sen—and some landscapes by KK himself adorned its walls.

The floors were covered with intricately woven carpets from Kashmir and Mirzapur. There was a divan with comfortable cushions and a large bolster, and little decoration except for one or two old and beautiful pieces of silver. Guests would find a continental meal cooked to perfection and elegantly served in Wedgewood china one day, only to be greeted on the next by an authentic Indian meal served on plates in a combination of gleaming black stoneware and silver.

Boruna's tanpura and piano found pride of place in her living room, for she was adept at playing both, having been trained by Dilip Kumar Roy, the famous founder of the Bengali 'raag-prodhan', an exquisite combination of the classical and the popular, and later by Monsieur Sondre of the Calcutta School of Music. Margaret, the wife of the local civil surgeon, accompanied Boruna at chamber concerts that helped to while away the long, cold winter evenings warmed by log fires in the grates.

And, of course, as Boruna well knew, an Englishwoman's real domain was the garden; for, the *'jardin Anglais'* had not only revolutionized French styles in the eighteenth century, courtesy Marie Antoinette, but had made serious inroads into the Mughal garden styles which had characterized the Indian scene till then. Boruna's efforts at creating the exquisite Eden to which we've already been introduced had been aided and given form by Mrs Margery Tucker, wife of the Divisional Superintendent of the railways in Muradabad. Margery, after twenty years in India, was still very much the memsahib: proud, haughty, with a biting sense of humour and a tongue with a cutting edge. People said, behind her back, that she was the one who wore the pants in her household, for her husband, Owen, was more a man of letters than a bureaucrat and spent all his spare time reading and writing poetry. For some reason, Margery had taken a fancy to Boruna from their very first meeting. Under their joint care, the garden had flourished well beyond Boruna's initial expectations.

In 1941, the political situation was turbulent, not only in India, at the height of the nationalist movement under Gandhiji's leadership, but right across Europe caught in the throes of the Second World War. With the 'Quit India' movement in the offing, many educated Indians in government service were facing an identity crisis. With the circulation of constant rumours that many people had become actively involved in underground activity and arms and ammunition were being moved around between cities, it became imperative for the British to secure the loyalty of their Indian officers.

Muradabad, a scene of ceaseless activity, was kept under close surveillance by the British government. A particularly rabid Englishman by the name of Geoffrey Hague had recently been given charge of the district administration. He was ably assisted by the Inspector General of Police, Swanson, and together they took pride in showing no mercy to those convicted or even suspected of any clandestine activity. The Union Jack fluttered proudly atop their homes and the Indian servants who worked for them were treated like dirt and replaced frequently.

KK and Boruna, by virtue of his position and her popularity, were compelled to attend frequent dinner parties at Hague's residence, a rare honour for a native but one that this couple could have done without. What

Boruna found particularly irksome was a custom scrupulously followed before the guests sat down to dinner: at every party all the guests would have to stand rigidly at attention round the dining table while the army band, complete with bagpipes, marched around the room, playing *'God save the King'*. Only then could the guests sit down to the dubious pleasures of a frugal and usually ill-cooked meal.

Hague took himself and his lineage, rumoured to be aristocratic, rather seriously and was very particular about the company he kept. Being a bachelor, he was courted assiduously by the few single women around, particularly the Tuckers' daughter, Alison. Pretty Mrs Sullivan, the wife of a Salvation Army major, enjoyed flirting with him and openly encouraged his advances. All this adulation had only made Hague more insufferable and convinced him that he was the answer to every young woman's prayer. Then, the Mukerjis had appeared on the scene. Hague found that the pretty Indian lady was quite impervious to his charm, and her husband could beat him solidly at chess, bridge and even tennis. Chagrined but intrigued, piqued but still fascinated, Hague had worked steadily at their capitulation, but so far had achieved very little success. As a matter of fact, holding his own in conversation with them was difficult enough, for both husband and wife had mastered the art of quick repartee.

KK's sister's son, Nabendu Chakravarti, had recently joined the provincial Civil Service and had come to Muradabad as Deputy Magistrate. Much to Boruna's delight, he had decided to stay with them. KK's three-year-old daughter, was particularly happy because she now had a playmate besides her father who would join her in imaginary exploits against demons, tell her stories about her favourite animals and take her for walks around the garden. A fine sportsman and mountaineer, suave and witty, and excellent at his work, Nabendu proved to be a godsend for Hague. Increasingly, Hague began to delegate his own work to the young man, even in the most sensitive areas, and indulged himself in his love for music, sport and shikar.

The year 1942 was to be a memorable one for India. The sense of outrage that Indians had felt at being drawn into Britain's war effort without their knowledge or consent, was steadily mounting, and was to find expression in an open challenge—'*Bharat choro*', quit India. People of every province were mobilized and the plan was to seize control of certain key towns to show the British that the Empire was worm-eaten and tottering on its foundations. Dinajpur in Bengal, Kanthi, Tamralipti and Satara in Maharashtra, and Azamgarh and Balia in the United Provinces, were to set up independent administrations to demonstrate that they could stand on their own feet and solve their own problems. Transferring of men and arms to these nodal points was done mainly through the railways, and KK and his nephew were deeply involved in the covert activities. Since this involved a fair amount of travelling, it was left to Boruna to cover their inexplicable absences and make up for their solecisms.

KK's frequent trips home to Allahabad through July 1942 due to his father's failing health had enabled him to carry out many duties without fear of detection. But after his father's death in August, during the crucial months when the insurgents were to carry out their plans, it was practically impossible for government servants to leave their posts as they were expected to be on duty twenty-four hours of the day. The very plans they had been helping to implement were now in danger of falling through. More so because Hague and Swanson had become very active and vigilant and saw to it that their subordinates toed the line.

A few weeks later Nabendu was entrusted with a particularly urgent mission. KK and he would have to supervise the transfer of a cache of arms at a point about seventeen kilometres beyond Muradabad, where a train would make an unscheduled stop because a certain passenger would pull the emergency chain. The consignment would be placed in Nabendu's jeep and in the pandemonium that was sure to ensue after the train stopped the arms would be transferred to a goods carriage and be delivered to Azamgarh the next morning. This particular train had been selected because it was scheduled to carry money from the British treasury. While this would provide Nabendu the chance to board the train when it passed without arousing any suspicion, it also meant that he would need to contend with extra security and would require KK's assistance and backup.

As luck would have it, Hague had decided to celebrate his birthday at his residence on the very same night. The two men were at their wits' end. While the train was scheduled to stop at 8.30 p.m. sharp, the party was to begin at 8.00 p.m. And if Hague, a stickler for punctuality, were to check with their respective departments and find them both out on 'unscheduled missions', he would smell a rat.

They turned to Boruna, 'You'll have to go to the party, Boruna. Only you can bail us out now.'

Though well aware of Hague's reputation with women, and a little apprehensive that KK would not be by her side, Boruna assured them of her cooperation. 'You'd better have a good story to tell them when you do turn up, or else . . .' she said.

Finally, they decided that it would be too risky to cut it so fine and they should take up independent assignments that evening. KK told Mr Tucker that to ensure that the train passed safely, he would follow it on his trolley for a part of the way. This was a hazardous enterprise for the push-trolley was a dangerous contraption. Essentially just a platform on wheels with guard rails, it had to be pushed along the railway track by four men who would run on the rails till the trolley picked up momentum and then jump on. Usually the vehicle acquired a velocity that allowed it to run for over a mile on its own. Then it had to be pushed again. This trolley was normally used for inspections during the day, but at night, in the biting cold and with wind-speeds of a 100 miles per hour, lit by a single swaying lantern, the experience could be intimidating. Mr Tucker, impressed by KK's dedication to duty, granted him permission on the spot and promised that he would inform the DM of his inability to attend the party. Two days later, Nabendu went to Hague with the offer to accompany the train in his jeep for security reasons, thus placing the ball neatly in Hague's court. Caught in the crossfire of personal vanity and duty Hague agreed, but stipulated that Nabendu would have to put in an appearance at the party, however late it was.

Everybody who was anybody in Muradabad was invited to Hague's party. For weeks the ladies had been planning what clothes and jewellery they would wear, and servants had been bribed to find out what the others would be wearing. Not particularly subtle in her dealings, Mrs Sullivan arrived at Boruna's doorstep, and inquired without any prelude, 'What are you wearing to Geoffrey's party?'

Boruna said that she really hadn't thought about it, but would probably wear white as KK thought it suited her best.

Visibly dismayed, Mrs Sullivan exclaimed, 'But I was planning on wearing white, and if you do, Geoff won't look at anybody else.'

As Mrs Tucker, who had been helping Boruna tend her plants, fumed under her breath at the woman's audacity, Boruna replied with a smile that she had no intention of stealing the limelight and would happily wear black even though it was her least favourite colour. Mrs Sullivan was ecstatic. She gave Boruna a hug, called her an angel and left.

'Really, Boruna. It amazes me how you can keep your cool,' Mrs Tucker burst out. 'Just let me spread the word around among these silly women, and we'll see who's wearing black and who's wearing white to the party!'

That evening, as Boruna dressed for the party the knot of fear in her heart refused to go away. The premonition of disaster that her morning prayers had failed to dispel still clung to her, and as she looked at herself in the triptych of mirrors on the dressing table, she found herself wishing that she were less attractive. It dawned on her that physical beauty was not an unmixed blessing, and that she would be quite vulnerable without KK beside her. She clutched her daughter to her heart for a moment before leaving and instructed the ayah that should she not return by 10 p.m. the maid should send one of the guards over to Hague's residence with an urgent message for her to return home.

Hague was standing on the steps receiving guests when Boruna drove up in her Vauxhall. He escorted her into the drawing room, where the guests had gathered. The women, all clad in white, made a great show of receiving her, wondering to themselves how it was that all of them were dressed in white while Boruna stood resplendent in shimmering black silk and gold jewellery. As the evening advanced and the level of inebriation mounted, Boruna found herself the cynosure of Hague's attention. He was constantly at her side, insisting on a dance whenever possible and even demanded that she lead the chorus in the birthday greeting.

The evening dragged on, and Boruna tried very hard not to look at the door too often. Surely, Nobu at least should have been back by now. A sinking feeling threatened to overwhelm her and she had terrible visions of both men in handcuffs, or worse. All the while, she continued to smile and did her best to participate in the inane and slightly bawdy conversations. Finally, when she could bear it no longer, she told her host she was tired and would like to go home. To her horror, Hague insisted on seeing her home, gallantly asserting that he would not allow Boruna to drive alone at this hour. What would KK say if he did?

Realizing that arguments would be of no use she agreed, but only on condition that Hague would take his own car, follow her home and return to his guests who showed no signs of leaving. Reluctantly, Hague promised his guests he would be back in half an hour, and followed her car down the paved, moonlit road.

When the Vauxhall purred into the portico with the Morris close behind, and Boruna jumped out of the car to wave goodbye, Hague was determined to see her into the house. He followed her to the sitting room, planted himself on the sofa and said, 'Won't you offer your friend a drink?'

Boruna retorted sharply that he'd had quite enough to drink for one night.

Hague's eyes began to glaze over. He looked at her and said, with an asinine giggle, 'Then give me a kiss, sweetheart, and I promise to leave.'

Boruna quietly moved away to the other end of the room. As Hague rose groggily to follow her, he collapsed in a heap on the carpet.

At this juncture, Boruna's little daughter walked into the room, rubbing her eyes and calling out for her mother to give her some water. She took one look at the prostrate Englishman, walked up to him and asked, 'Uncle Hague, you fell down? You want medicine?'

And that is how KK and Nabendu found them a moment or two later: the child, with a serious and concerned face, bending over Hague, and Boruna laughing helplessly at the other end of the room!

It seemed that their plans had gone awry to begin with, for the train had travelled much further than scheduled because the collaborator who was supposed to pull the chain had fallen asleep. When the train had finally stopped, a group of men had darted away from a carriage and many of the policemen had run after them under the misapprehension that they were thieves. By the time it had been established that they were merely answering an urgent call of nature, the transfer of arms had been made. However, the process of checking had gone on for some time, for Nabendu had been punctilious in his duty. KK and his men had then returned by the trolley, and it had taken him fifteen minutes to run home from the station.

At the party, Swanson was beginning to get restive, when KK appeared on the scene supporting the still groggy Hague. He announced solemnly to the assembled party that Mr Hague had been taken ill and required medical attention. The civil surgeon, an intelligent man, made a big show of examining him and advised that he be put to bed, and the party slowly broke up.

When Nabendu turned up at Hague's residence the next morning, with flowers to wish him a speedy recovery, he carried an anxious inquiry from the Mukerjis and a get-well card. The cache of arms reached Azamgarh and was carried safely to its destination, and both Swanson and Hague accepted Nabendu's lengthy and graphically detailed report without a murmur!

Years later, when Boruna's favourite granddaughter, watching her lay out shiny silver cutlery on the dining table, dubbed her 'the last bastion of the British Empire', Boruna made her sit on a stool at her feet and recounted the story of *her* contribution to the country's struggle for freedom.

1945

The Trial

'THE LOVED ONE ... THAT'S WHAT YOUR NAME MEANS, DULARI,' the man says to the shy, five-year-old girl standing a few feet away, tracing designs in the dust with her toe. The man is a stranger to the village. He appeared out of the blue about six months ago and had made a deserted shrine his home though the collapsing structure was rumoured to be haunted. An ancient banyan tree has spread its buttress roots through the broken brickwork and created a shelter of sorts. The villagers, awed by his courage, leave him alone but some of them are drawn to him by his golden voice. In the deep of night, while the village sleeps, the man sits next to a twig fire and sings the immortal words of Kabir to the stars.

> Take heed, O proud one,
> Before there is no one left to keep you company ...
> Youth is spent in search of learning and wealth,
> Manhood is wasted in woman-games,
> Old age looks back at innocent childhood
> and repents endlessly ...
> No one keeps you company till the end,
> Least of all your dreams and illusions.

To Dulari, lying awake on the floor of her hut while her brother sleeps peacefully in their mother's arms on a string cot in a corner, the wondrous melody brings the realization that human voices can be beautiful, just like the songs of birds and the rustling of the wind in the tall grass and the leaves; that they do not find expression in reprimand, abuse and altercation alone. Dulari is drawn irresistibly to the man, who makes up little rhymes for her, shows her how to make a fire with a piece of glass, and tells her stories from the *Ramayana* and the *Purana*s and about brave women like Rani Lakshmibai of Jhansi. In the somnolent afternoons, when the household chores are done and her brother is asleep, she creeps to the cool shade of the banyan and loses count of time as she listens to his stories and his songs.

One day she asks him, 'Will you teach me how to read?'

Delighted, he procures a slate and pencil and proceeds to teach her. Within a week, she has mastered the alphabet and the matras, in the second week she learns how to join letters to form diphthongs and in the week after that she is reading and writing with reasonable fluency. When it comes to learning, her appetite is insatiable. She races through the books he gives her and clamours for more.

One afternoon she falls down and twists her ankle. He takes her swollen foot in his hand and explains exactly why she feels so much pain. With deft fingers he rubs the area with kerosene oil from a lamp. Dulari walks home with scarcely a limp and the rudiments of the art of massage etched in her mind. Later, she will perfect the skill and use it to earn money to keep herself and her four children fed and clothed.

Dulari is fifteen now. Her friend has been gone for some time and there is no news of him. It happens all the time: he disappears like a shadow and returns after weeks as though he had never left. Curious villagers have tried their best to discover his antecedents and find out what he does and where he goes, but to little avail. They agree, though, that he is 'not a bad fellow' and that he is generous with the little money he has. But this time Dulari is not waiting for him to return. Other, larger concerns have found their way into her life.

In 1942, the much-dreaded famine is doing the rounds of the villages and, with the war effort at its height, the British government has little inclination or time to pay heed to the woes of poor 'natives'. To make matters worse, people are hoarding wheat, bajra and jowar in the hope of future gain, which only adds to the misery. In Dulari's house, all the real food is saved for her drunken father and her spoilt brat of a brother. Her mother, sister—Mohini—and she survive mainly on sweet potato that needs very little water to grow. Boiled or baked, it is the staple food in any case but it can become monotonous if eaten three times a day, for weeks on end. Finally, when sweet potato is no longer available and starvation stares the village in the face, the great exodus begins. Winding lines of emaciated people, their pathetic possessions tied in little bundles on their heads, move like automatons towards the nearest town in a desperate attempt to survive. There they hope to engage in long and back-breaking labour for a pittance or to beg pitifully for some of the water drained from the rice that the townspeople have cooked.

Dulari's family is headed for Munger, a town in north Bihar on the banks of the Ganga with its famous Kashtharini ghat which, as its name suggests, 'alleviates pain'. Sita was supposed to have rested here on her travels with Ram and Lakshman. A large, squarish stone under a peepal tree near the ghat bears the imprint of her delicate feet. Strange, that in the land where Sita is so greatly revered, women should be treated so cruelly. But then, Sita too became an icon only after a lifetime of travail and ignominy: an icon of the subservient, all-suffering and patient woman. Men have seen to it that only these among her many qualities are always highlighted, while her courage, outrage and revolt are hardly spoken about.

Munger is a good hundred miles away from Dulari's village and, starved as they are, Dulari and her family find it impossible to walk more than four or five miles a day. Increasingly, their path is lined with swollen and grotesque bodies of men and animals in varying stages of decay. Water is scarce and often they have to drink liquid mud to quench their thirst. Strangely enough, unlike the last journey of the Pandavas in the *Mahabharata* where the 'weak woman' Draupadi fell first, it is Dulari's big, drunken bully of a father who succumbs. He dies with his head in his wife's lap. His daughters, whom he has abused steadily throughout his life, physically and mentally, do their best to keep the flies off, while his son, thirteen years old, selfish and self-centred, looks on passively till his mother implores him to pour some water into the dying man's mouth. And so, another body is added to the steadily growing tally on the roadside.

Exhausted, mother and daughters sleep like logs under a tree and come to only when the scorching sun, climbing steadily in the sky, makes the ground so hot it burns their skin. Dulari's brother is nowhere to be seen. Assuming that he has stepped away to speak to someone, they wait like inert puppets, lacking the volition to think or plan. Two hours pass, but her brother does not return. They inquire of other skeletal figures who pass by, but receive only blank stares in response. Suddenly, a terrible suspicion grips Dulari and she fumbles in her mother's purse to discover that it has been cleared of its last coin— just what she had dreaded. The scion of the house has disappeared to save his own precious hide, leaving the women to their fate. Dulari's mother, her body worn from years of incessant labour and inadequate nutrition, is unable to bear the shock and collapses by the roadside a few days later. Almost a fortnight after that, two skeletons, vaguely reminiscent of Dulari and Mohini, fall at their maternal uncle's feet in a shanty on the outskirts of Munger.

Chandar Das is a kindly man and does not think twice about taking the girls in despite having five children of his own. When his wife remonstrates, he tells her to feed them properly so that they can start earning and contributing towards the daily expenses. He works as a gardener in Basdeopur, a neighbouring village, where the Imperial Tobacco Company has a large factory and a residential colony for its management staff and their families. Laid out on a hundred acres of undulating land, beautifully landscaped, with a lake, paved, winding roads, tall flowering trees, bungalows with exquisite gardens, a large clubhouse equipped with a swimming pool, tennis courts, bowling alleys and a cricket field, it is a little paradise, totally incongruous, particularly at the time, with its environs. The easy cultivation of indigo that the

land afforded, had initially attracted British merchants
to this area. Then they began to cultivate tobacco and
the cheap labour, abundantly available, added to the lure.
Imperial Tobacco had subsequently set up its
manufacturing unit here.

Chandar earns an inconceivable salary of fifty rupees
a month. He is also allowed to carry away the grass he
mows at the end of the day to feed his cows. A handsome
giant of a man, well over six feet in height, clad in a
short dhoti and a baniyan and with a touch of silver at
his throat, he carries the bundle weighing over forty
pounds on his head with the easy grace of a dancer. Life
has been good to him and since he has always had a soft
corner for his unfortunate sister who had been married
off to a brute of a man at the tender age of eight, he now
welcomes the opportunity to help her daughters in
whatever way he can.

A month passes. With wholesome food in their
bellies, a touch of oil on rough skin and pared nails, the
two girls undergo a magical transformation. The shadow
of impending death has also lifted from their lives with
the inkling of hope of a decent future. Mohini, at
seventeen, is just as beautiful as her name suggests, and
is ready for marriage. Chandar and his wife decide to
keep her at home to help with the household chores
while they look out for a suitable groom who will

hopefully, enchanted by her, not demand too much dowry. But Dulari, tall and thin, with a mass of unruly hair on her head and an interesting rather than beautiful face, amazingly literate and well spoken, they decide to place in domestic service.

Chandar's inquiries reveal that the Carters, a young English couple with a two-year-old son and the wife expecting again, are on the lookout for a suitable ayah. They have been 'interviewing' for some time but have found no one among the local women they particularly like. So when Dulari, modestly but neatly turned out, hair firmly plaited, feet and hands scrupulously clean, intelligent, pleasant and demure, turns up at their doorstep, she is an immediate hit. Mrs Carter takes her on for a seven-day trial and finds that little Gary is attracted to her instantly. Dulari plays games with him, helps him make kites and restricts him to a strict routine as far as his meals, play time and naps are concerned. After a lifetime of babysitting, this is child's play for her. Also, she keeps to the nursery and the garden with Gary and never intrudes when the family is together. Mrs Carter, in her fifth month of pregnancy, relieved that she does not need to worry about Gary, confirms Dulari in service at the end of the week for twenty-five rupees a month and a Christmas bonus of fifty rupees. For Dulari, who has never had a rupee to call her own, this is indeed an extraordinary fortune. She dutifully hands over her salary to her uncle every month and manages her personal expenses with the bakshish she gets from visiting guests or from her mistress for doing some extra work. Mr Carter's mother once gave her five whole rupees on one of her visits for massaging her back and an evening's relief from the nagging rheumatic pain. Dulari only spends on essentials and saves the rest in a small purse that she hides under her mattress. Every morning when she wakes up she cannot help feeling that her life is a dream from which she will suddenly awake to her old life of squalid horror.

The months fly by and soon Dulari completes a year with the Carters. Gary is three now, and an English nanny arrives to take charge of his education. Mary Clarkson is a plain spinster, about thirty-five, educated but not overburdened with imagination, and when Gary completes his lessons he runs out to the garden to chase imaginary tigers and robbers with Dulari. In the meantime, Gary's eight-month-old sister, Betty, demands much of Dulari's attention.

One day, Dulari asks Mary if she will teach her English. With Mrs Carter's permission, Mary gives Dulari English lessons for half an hour in the evenings after the children have fallen asleep. Like Dulari's erstwhile friend, she too is amazed at the rapidity with which the girl masters not only the rudiments of the written language but speech skills as well. In a couple of months, the Carters find Dulari speaking to the children in fairly correct, short sentences in a clipped British accent. When Chandar hints that Dulari is now of marriageable age and that he will have to start looking for a groom, they protest vociferously. When they leave Basdeopur on transfer, they will leave Dulari enough money for a decent alliance, they say. And so, Dulari gets a reprieve of another two years.

At the Carters, Dulari also becomes aware of how the members of the upper crust live. Their values, she notices, are very different. Kindness and honesty are not luxuries for them, but everyday norms, and these people are good not because they hope to get something out of it but because that is the way they are. Her faith in fellow human beings that her friend had once inspired in her is renewed. Slowly, the spectres of yesteryears recede and Dulari becomes a confident, happy person, content with her life and herself.

Another year goes by. One winter morning Dulari picks up the newspaper casually, and is brought up short by a photograph on the front page. Older, thinner, bearded but unmistakable, it is her 'friend'. However, this is no ordinary situation, for he is clearly behind bars, and the photographer has caught a glimpse of him through the grill. She tries to read the article that follows but the letters swirl before her eyes and refuse to resolve themselves into words. Finally, she goes to Mary who reads it aloud in her unemotional voice: 'Shubhankar Jha, the well-known terrorist who has been involved in countless attacks on British officers and institutions, has finally been arrested. He is in Munger Jail awaiting trial. He has escaped from jail before. Special precautions have been taken for his protection. Congress leaders have made a special request for consideration but, given his record, there is little possibility of the British government acceding.'

Dulari stands, stricken, unable to comprehend fully the purport of Mary's words. She excuses herself, requests Mary to keep an eye on the children and withdraws to her room. Slowly, as she regains composure, she is able to make sense of the whole affair. She realizes now why Shubhankar had led such a private life, chosen their remote village as his home and disappeared for such long spells. She also realizes that when he spoke so affectionately of his 'mother', as he did very often with a passion that had sometimes made her jealous, he had meant his country, his motherland.

Memories of the time she spent with him surge in her head: his mellow voice reciting poems he made up for her, telling her stories, his gentle touch . . . She closes her eyes tightly as realization washes over her like a flood. In her utter need and loneliness she had been prepared to surrender to him completely, but instead of taking advantage of the situation he had turned her face to the light, away from the darkness that had threatened to engulf her. Instantly, her mind is made up: the debt must be repaid.

But how can she do it? The absurdity of the situation, that she—a slip of a girl—would, in effect, be pitting herself against the might of the Empire, never strikes her; she is too busy planning. First, she decides, she needs an ally. Her uncle she rejects outright—too good and honest, he might not prove too useful. The Carters will not be able to help her even if they wanted to. They are good friends of the District Magistrate and the police chief, and the sense of racial fraternity is too strong. Then an idea comes to her. Of course! Shambhudada, the head of the guards in the Basdeopur Colony—he is the only man who can help her.

Munger, an old town, had been the scene of political activity from as far back as the time of Mir Jaffer and Mir Kasim, Muslim feudal lords of the eighteenth century. In 1765, when the British took over the tax collection of Bihar, Bengal and Orissa, the power of the Muslim rulers had gradually eroded but the groups formed on the basis of castes and clans continued to flourish and fight among themselves over property, influence, women and money. Ordinary people lived in great fear of these factions and dubbed them 'dacoits'. But the British merchants always kept on their right side and enjoyed their protection. When the British in turn established 'law and order', the power of these clans was reduced and some members even sought employment with their erstwhile protégés. The Imperial Tobacco Company's security service in Basdeopur factory was therefore managed by a family of stalwarts and headed by Shambhudada.

When Shambhu, a giant of a man with huge handlebar moustache walks around with his well-oiled bamboo stave in his hand, calling out *'Jagte raho!'* in the dead of night, the earth seems to tremble. People in the colony sleep with their windows wide open and doors merely latched, secure in the knowledge that Shambhu and his clan are on the prowl. Owing to his antecedents and connections, Shambhu is a powerful man and has many friends in the police force; Dulari is sure he will know how to get her to Jha.

That evening, when the Carter children are asleep, Dulari creeps out of the house and goes to the main gatehouse, where Shambhu allocates duties and arranges the watch. She waits till he has arranged things to his satisfaction, then she seats herself at his feet and comes out with her appeal. Shambhu is taken aback. He knows a good deal about Jha and his activities. In fact, he had been a part of the network many years ago and admires him greatly even now. But he has sworn loyalty to his masters and will not do anything to betray their trust. To be a *namakharam* is unthinkable. But he also knows Dulari; she will not take no for an answer. So he shrugs his massive shoulders and tells her that he knows the head constable at the jail and will give Dulari a letter of introduction. After that it will be her game.

When Dulari asks Mrs Carter for a week's leave to visit her sister, Mohini, who is expecting a baby, no one has any suspicions, and the following morning Dulari finds herself in Munger.

The gaol in Munger, adjacent to the courthouse, is more in the nature of a lockup. Keeping in mind the importance of the prisoner, four extra policemen have been deployed on a twenty-four-hour vigil. Aware of Jha's political connections and popular appeal, the administration is anxious to expedite the trial, but getting people to testify against Jha has not been easy.

Opposite the courthouse is a tea shop, a makeshift affair of bamboo and corrugated tin, popular for its deliciously rich elaichi chai. Two chulhas burn constantly, stoked by four small boys. Each has a cauldron on it to boil water and milk separately. The tea leaves are boiled in a third cauldron which contains a mixture of milk and water heavily laced with sugar and cardamom, and is managed by the owner himself. Sweet, thick and rich, it is an invigorating beverage served in small cups made of baked mud. Wooden benches are scattered around the shop and provide an ideal opportunity for idlers and observers who wish to watch the proceedings of the courthouse. Women who frequent the shop are usually relatives of incarcerated people and are treated with compassion. So when Dulari sits on a bench and gingerly sips her tea, she does not cause too much of a stir. Her uncle is in the lockup, she tells those who ask and few attempt to probe further.

Jha is naturally the subject of much debate and discussion and as Dulari listens she is heartened to find that the speakers are strongly in his favour. They are especially critical of the fact that he has been detained here like a common criminal, instead of being accorded the status of a 'Rajbandi', a prisoner of state, and being placed under house arrest. However, many feel that after Subhas Bose's spectacular escape from his residence in Calcutta the British government cannot afford to take such chances. Comments are lobbed back and forth like a ping-pong ball and the loud sipping of tea provides a ready chorus.

A young man who has been sitting quietly, sipping his tea and listening avidly to the conversation, interpolates a question or two subtly aimed at discovering the duration of the watches, the times at which the personnel change and, particularly, the identity of the head constable who makes these arrangements. An older man joins the group sometime later, and though they continue to participate in the conversation it is clear to Dulari, who has been watching them closely, that they are more interested in speaking to each other. When they leave she follows them discreetly at a distance, catching up with them as they hit a deserted stretch of road.

'Ram Ram babuji,' she greets them.

Instantly suspicious, they try to brush her off, but she persists, 'You must listen to me! It is a matter of life and death.'

Arrested by the sincerity in her voice and the appeal in her eyes, they finally stop to hear her out. Dulari then tells them about her acquaintance with Jha, mentioning places and times, elaborating on his kindness and generosity and her admiration and affection for him. But she assiduously suppresses her present employment and residence. They question her closely and promise to meet her at the tea shop the next day.

At 8.00 a.m. the next day the men are nowhere to be seen around the tea shop. Dulari's heart sinks as time passes and they do not appear. She is seriously considering an alternative course of action, clasping in her closed fist the letter from Shambhu to the head constable, when the men appear. They take no notice of her and proceed to drink their tea and talk to the others. But when they get up to leave, they signal her to follow. Today, when they speak to her, she is taken aback by the warmth of their greeting. They lead her to a deserted shanty and settle down to do some serious planning. It seems time is at a premium. Copious bribery has produced witnesses whose testimonies will incriminate Jha on charges of arson, loot and murder. The trial will be brief and vicious. The end will come early in the morning on the scaffold before the town stirs.

Dulari is close to tears now. 'Is there nothing that can be done?' she asks them. Hesistantly they tell her that there might just be a chance of arranging an escape, but only if she agrees to play a vital part. There is a man on the night-watch who may be persuaded into keeping the other guards away for one night and being knocked unconscious by Jha with his handcuffs, by going too near the grill. Once he is out of the way, Jha will pick the padlock and escape. But . . .

'But what?' Dulari almost screams.

The head constable—a vicious man, a sadist and a womanizer of the worst order—has a personal grudge against Jha and will never allow this to happen, unless . . . Dulari eagerly breaks in, saying that she has a letter from a friend of the head constable and can easily strike up an acquaintance with him and ask him for help.

The two men exchange glances. They are not equipped to deal with such innocent enthusiasm, such clear-eyed sincerity. Brusquely, the older man turns away, taps the other on the shoulder and says, 'Enough, let's go.'

They rise to leave, but Dulari bars their way. 'Have I done something wrong?' she implores. 'Are you annoyed with me? Why won't you tell me what I can do?'

They still hesitate but she is adamant and, finally, the whole sordid truth comes out: striking up an acquaintance with the havildar will mean a close liaison with him, and the only way she can distract him on the night of the escape is by...

They are too embarrassed to go on. But they have no conception of Dulari's stark realism, no idea of how and in what circumstances her childhood has been spent. They do not realize that to her sex is not coloured by romanticism; it merely represents power. If that power can help the one man who has shown her the light, so be it.

'You fix the date. I will take care of the havildar,' she tells them.

But, in the quiet of the night, doubts assail her. She has seen the worst—her drunken father's nightly assaults on her whimpering mother, heavy with child or on her bad days, a ten-year-old gang-raped to death, repeated acts of incest. In her own awakening sexuality she recognized that a woman's body is her greatest power and vulnerability, and she had often wondered about the role sex would play in her own life. The last few years have changed that. The Carters have shown her that a man—woman relationship is just as much about companionship, as has the strong partnership her uncle and aunt share; and now Mohini, glowing and content ever since she has been married, is expecting her first child.

Dulari realizes that there is no reason to treat what is to come as a tragedy. This is a job that must be done; she will do her duty and then carry on as usual. A sudden memory from her childhood comes to her aid: there had been a cholera epidemic in her village and many, including two of her close friends, had died from the disease. Inconsolable, she had sought out Jha. He had stroked her hair till she had stopped sobbing, and told her, 'Don't be afraid of death. Death is not final. Just as you change your old clothes and wear new ones, so you shed one body to enter another. The soul, the real you, never dies.' Since the body is merely the outer clothing of the soul, she reasons, the abuse of her body would never touch the real Dulari. After this she sleeps like a child and wakes with renewed determination on the morrow.

The next night, dressed in a bright red and yellow lehnga—choli she stands on the havildar's doorstep, letter from Shambhudada in hand. From that moment, things move fast. Dulari weaves such a web of sensuality around the rotten man that he loses all sense of time and place. The night Shubhankar Jha escapes is the culmination of the havildar's seven-day aphrodisiac dream.

On a crystal-clear morning Dulari walks straight to Kashtharini ghat, where the Ganga had once solaced Sita. She remains in the water till she feels she has cleansed her body of all corruption and that it belongs to her again. Then she wears fresh clothes and turns to the sun, fervently praying that she be absolved of her sins.

> God of Light, thou seest all,
> Look into my heart and absolve me.
> Just as thy purity is daily renewed and darkness
>   dispelled,
> So may my heart and soul be cleansed of evil
> By thy light and power.
> And when I return to life, to love,
> May I do so untainted, uncorrupted.

Though her eyes are closed the light seems to blind her. She feels the sun's powerful beams piercing her skin, entering her body through her pores, soaking up the darkness in her heart, pervading her entire being. Then the light slowly recedes and a curious sense of peace lightens Dulari's heart.

She goes to Mohini's house to pick up her things. Mohini is loath to let her go and Dulari promises to return for the birth of the baby. Then she heads back to Basdeopur to pick up life where she had left off a week before.

1956

Motherhood

ONCE A PRINCELY STATE, REWA IN NORTHERN MADHYA PRADESH is an area that is full of gorges, valleys, tumbling waterfalls, swift-flowing streams and huge boulders. Local legend has it that ceaseless wars, private feuds, countless murders, fratricide, parricide and infanticide have caused so much bloodshed through the centuries that the soil in this region has turned red. In the rays of the setting sun, the entire landscape, earth and water, looks as though it is on fire.

This arid land was home to the Thakurs who dominated rural society, even in British India. Wealthy and powerful, the Thakurs were reminiscent of the feudal barons of medieval England and Europe in their zest for life, uneasy spirituality, capacity for unspeakable cruelty and unexpected generosity. They ruled their estates with an iron hand and the people who served them were terrified of their masters. But they were also fiercely protective of their subjects and would fight tooth and nail for them, whether the enemies were robbers, tigers or neighbouring rulers.

The power nexus of crown and altar is an ancient one and Rewa was no exception. Located near the Vindhya mountains with the famous Vindhyavasini and Ashtabhuja temples, Rewa had its own share of gods, shrines and Brahmins, the priests whose word was law, for they held the keys to the kingdom of heaven and regulated entry into the realms of the gods. Every third banyan tree in the state had a platform built around it that sported a few stones and pebbles of uncertain lineage covered with sindur. The local priest claimed that these stones had astounding supernatural powers. Myths had been skilfully woven around them and the gullible villagers gave up a fair portion of their meagre earnings to propitiate their local deities, keeping the priest and his family in comfort. Coincidences, shrewdly engineered, bolstered their faith and fuelled the fear that lay just beneath the surface.

When Jaggu, the local iconoclast, refused to pay homage and his son died of snakebite a day later, he and the villagers saw only nemesis at work. Jaggu repented and returned to the fold, completely unaware that the snake belonged to the private collection of the pujari. In fact, anyone who was bitten by a snake was taken not to a doctor but to the priest, who doubled as the medicine man with occult powers. The unconscious victim would be laid down on the platform under the banyan tree and his relatives asked to keep a respectful distance. Seven lamps would then be lit and placed around the man's head and a bowl of milk kept at his feet. Then the pujari would take out a knife and slit a vein close to the bite. As the blood began to flow, the priest would chant mantras which were always beyond the comprehension of the terrified onlookers. The villagers would watch in awe and dread as a snake emerged from the darkness, slithered past the supine form and began to drink from the bowl. Meanwhile, the chanting would continue and the audience waited with bated breath for the faintest stirrings of life. When the snake finally moved away, back to the basket from which it has emerged, the priest would approach the stricken man and feel his pulse. If the bloodletting proved efficacious and the man survived, it was ascribed to the bounty of the 'king of snakes'. If the man died, it was because 'nagraj' was unsatisfied and further propitiation would be required. In either case, the villagers would be overwhelmed with gratitude for the selfless pujari who had stood by them in their hour of need, and cries of 'Jai Maharaj', 'Jai Nagraj' would fill the air.

Another day, Manglu's attractive wife was on her way back from the river where she had gone to fetch water. She walked gracefully along the stony path, three clay pots filled with water poised on her head, one on top of the other, back ramrod straight, hips swaying rhythmically, not a drop of water spilling from the brimming vessels. It was monsoon. Clouds had been rumbling all day, and as she reached a fork on the road, the heavens opened. Afraid of losing her footing on the slippery path and breaking the pots, she took shelter under a banyan tree. For a few minutes, she stood taking stock of her precarious position, trying to get the water out of her eyes. Then, as she lifted her arms to set the pots down, a pair of greedy hands clasped both her breasts from behind. Before she could cry out, a hand closed over her mouth and a man's voice hissed in her ear that he was the spirit of the tree, Barelu, and that he would not hurt her if she acceded to his desire. She stood, petrified, as the pots were lifted from her head. She was disrobed and laid down on the cold, wet ground. The face that loomed over her as she was penetrated was hideously daubed in black, red and green; but the body that raped her again and again was surprisingly human. After an hour, the rain showed signs of letting up and the 'spirit' too had had its fill. With dire warnings against disclosure, the figure slipped away into the trees, leaving her prostrate on the ground, her naked body plastered with mud and semen. Silent and trembling, she went back to the river, washed herself and her clothes and put them on. She retrieved the pots and walked home, her gait a travesty of its former majesty. Fortunately, Manglu was not at home and her mother-in-law was out visiting a neighbour. She felt no guilt, however, only a curious excitement that the spirit should have singled her out to satiate its desire. When she went to the temple the next day, for the Janamashtami celebrations, she failed to recognize the spectre in the benign pujari, who placed his hand on her head and uttered the traditional blessing,

'Bathe in milk, bear many offspring', even as his lips parted in a reminiscent smile.

In Rewa, there was a small village called Rikhiyan that nestled among bamboo groves, mango orchards, sisam trees and clumps of the ubiquitous babul. A deep gorge ran through the village and the stream that flowed at the bottom worked assiduously at deepening it even further. On both sides of this cleft were caves with the most exquisite idols of various deities. The caves had become a popular place of pilgrimage since people believed that all they wished for would be theirs if they prayed here. These caves were under the charge of a family of pujaris, the Mishras, who claimed lineage from one Jagannath Mishra who was said to have been blessed by Lord Ram himself. The clout they had was tremendous even as late as in the 1950s: even the raja had to seek their permission before he visited the caves to make his offerings.

The zamindars in this area were prosperous and enjoyed the support of the Mishra clan, who were also their *kulpurohits* or family priests. In turn, the Mishras enjoyed certain privileges which included their less reputable activities often being overlooked. The smaller farmers, most of whom were indebted to the priests, rendered unpaid service without a murmur; but the people who were completely at their mercy and entirely helpless were the *achhuts*, the untouchables. They lived

in ramshackle bamboo structures at one end of the village
and worked as farm labourers, artisans, cobblers and
scavengers, earning whatever little they could. Cert..in
sections of the village were completely out of bounds
for them. They were allowed to bathe only in a designated
spot in the river and could draw water from a lone well
in their area. Infringement of these rules could have
severe repercussions: severing of limbs, branding with
hot irons, cropping of ears and being paraded naked
around the village with everybody watching. The men
suffered more, but women were not spared and neither
were children. Up to their necks in debt with no hope
of a future for themselves or their progeny, they had
long lost the strength and the will to voice their protests.
However, on the rare occasions when things went too
far they would go completely berserk and always act
together. At that point arson, murder, rape, mutilation,
nothing lay beyond them and the magistrate had to
intervene with his police force. In post-Independence
India, the magistrate's verdict was not always palatable
to the Thakurs, for he tended to conclude that the
'untouchables' were more sinned against than sinning,
and the sentence passed was light. Gandhiji's
indefatigable campaign in defence of the untouchables
was beginning to leaven the solid crust of conservatism,
and the new officers of the Indian Administrative Service
were enlightened young men and women who refused

to make common cause with the oppressors. This had not changed the Thakurs' attitude, but made them more cautious and refined their cruelties. The cleverer ones began to pose as benefactors and exploitation flourished behind the facade of hypocrisy.

Holi, the festival of spring, was celebrated with the greatest gusto and excitement in the villages of Madhya Pradesh. After the rigours of winter, with the rabi crops safely harvested, young and old, rich and poor forgot their problems and gave themselves up to colour, music, dance and heady enjoyment. Even the dreary lives of the achhuts would be irradiated by this gaiety, and for two days they celebrated with complete abandon.

The festivities began the night before Holi with a bonfire, and young and old sang and danced around the fire till late into the night. Early next morning the children rushed about carrying packets of gulal, pichkaris and buckets full of coloured water. At noon, tired but content, everybody gathered under the trees and home-made sweets and large cauldrons of sherbet were brought out. This was no ordinary sherbet, however, for it contained siddhi, a mild derivative of marijuana. Under its influence people could neither stop laughing nor crying once they got started.

At this time the Mishra family put in an appearance. This was their way of creating an impression of benign bonhomie. They brought mats with them for they would touch nothing that belonged to the achhuts. They also brought some money which they would distribute to the children as a show of their magnanimity. It was on such an occasion that the head pujari's brother, Murari Mishra, spotted Heeriya, the daughter of Chhagan, one of the poorest in the poverty-stricken community. Because he suffered from tuberculosis, Chhagan was unable to put in the hard labour required to earn enough to keep body and soul together. His attractive wife had left him for another man, and Heeriya did whatever odd jobs came her way and sometimes went begging for a meal for her father and herself.

Murari called her up to take some money. She walked up shyly and didn't put out her hand till her father urged her to. The entire assembly stared, including Murari's elder brother, Damodar, as Murari put ten rupees in Heeriya's palm. Ten rupees! Chhagan tripped over his own feet in dismay. Realizing his excess, Murari turned to him. 'This is for your medicines and some milk,' he said quickly. 'I had no idea you were so unwell ... in future I will keep an eye on you.'

On their way home, Damodar warned Murari, 'Poverty is a bottomless well. There are too many Chhagans in this world. How many can you rescue? Besides, you are engaged to be married. You'll soon have a family of your own and plenty of responsibility. No sequel to the day's event, please.'

But try as he might, Murari could not get Chhagan's pain-racked face or its transformation on seeing the ten-rupee note out of his mind. What would happen to Heeriya when Chhagan died, he wondered. The plaintive eyes, the proud set of the head, the shy smile like the breaking of dawn—must they all end on the whore-heap? He approached his father. Couldn't they employ Heeriya to sweep the outer precincts of the temple and allow her to live in the broken hut next to the cowshed? Surely, the animals will not mind an untouchable sharing their space.

Murari's father, the patriarch of the family, had always known that he had spawned an odd one in Murari—instead of devoting his energies to his own salvation, he insisted on looking beyond. Their home had been a haven for wounded and sick animals when he was a child and now that he was in his mid-twenties human derelicts attracted him more. But, as a man of god, it would not be proper to refuse his appeal. So Heeriya was employed as a sweeper for ten rupees a month. However, she refused to leave her father and gladly walked eight miles a day to and from the temple.

Heeriya was an excellent worker, always ready to do anything she was told to and very soon she became a favourite with the temple staff. She arose every morning even before the sun came up, finished cooking for her father and left her hut by 4.00 a.m. By 8.00 a.m. every morning, before the pujaris arrived, she would finish sweeping the temple premises. Then she would cover the beaten soil of the panchvati, the sacred grove of five trees reserved for meditation, with liquid mud and cow dung, and scatter every corner of the temple with water from the Ganga to purify the area cleaned by her, a member of the lowest caste. More than grateful for the money she received at the end of the month, she did not consider any of this as hardship.

Chhagan lived longer than expected owing to the good food and medicines Heeriya was now able to bring home, but the disease was too far gone and ultimately claimed his life. As Heeriya watched her father's lifeless body burning on the pyre, she wondered what was to become of her now. When she returned from the burning ghat after the last rites, a servant from the Mishra household was waiting with the message that Murari's wife, Chandra, wanted to meet Heeriya. She made her way to the temple, her heart full of trepidation. But there was good news waiting for her. Chandra, who had no children of her own and had always treated Heeriya like her own child, had already arranged for a hut near the panchvati to be allocated to her so that she could move in without delay. Thus, Heeriya became a regular member of the temple staff, entitled to a place to stay and a regular salary.

Two years went by. Murari's father passed away and Damodar took his place. Heeriya was now seventeen years old, but as yet unmarried——an unthinkable state of affairs in this backward village. Chandra, who had been busy matchmaking for her, finally settled on Ramdas, a young basket-maker, who had lost his parents in a train accident some years ago. Since he had no settled home of his own, Ramdas came to live in Heeriya's quarters after their marriage.

Till now Heeriya had not known what it meant to be in love. Loyalty, gratitude, affection she could recognize, as she could resentment and even hatred. But this strange stirring in her heart and the yearning in her breasts when Ramdas's strong arms held her close were new to her. Unlike other girls of her age, there had been no promiscuity in her life. Her single-minded commitment to her father and their survival had precluded friendship, gossip, any kind of social interaction. Perhaps this was the reason for her fanatical attachment to Ramdas and her ecstatic joy at knowing that her feelings were reciprocated.

Ramdas himself was quite in awe of Heeriya. He marvelled at her quiet strength, her determination, her commitment to her work, and he did his best to live up to her expectations. Slowly, she weaned him away from toddy, the occasional bouts of gambling and the frequent drags at a hookah of tobacco and hashish. With Murari's permission, he began to sell his baskets outside the temple and soon set up a workshop and employed four young men to weave the baskets while he supervised their work and travelled to the bazaars in nearby villages to sell his wares. He always returned by nightfall, however, for he did not want Heeriya to be alone, even though Chandra promised she would take care of her. Heeriya was happy. She drank lustfully from the cup of life, not realizing the notorious fragility of the cup and the portentous character of the metaphor.

Meanwhile, radical changes were taking place in Madhya Pradesh of the 1960s. Growing awareness among the lower caste about what they had been deprived of for so long and the unequal treatment meted out to them by their 'betters' had brought into play feelings of deep resentment which had begun to find expression in acts of defiance and assertiveness. The words 'harijan' (people of god) and 'dalit' (downtrodden) had begun to replace the earlier demeaning 'achhut' and the lexical connotation was very clear. They began to demand education and opportunities to better their economic condition. They also realized that their large numbers constituted a valuable vote-bank that could be utilized to their advantage and had begun to make forays into the political arena.

The Thakurs and their Brahmin protégés quickly realized that too much was at stake for them in terms of prestige and financial gain. If the lower castes indeed revolted there would be no cheap or unpaid labour and no homage to thrive on. The Thakurs strengthened their private armies of lathials to quell any attempt at protest, propagating a reign of terror that was as psychologically damaging as it was physically brutal. Men, women and children became indiscriminate victims of these reprisals, further highlighting their vulnerability and proving to them how fragile their newfound attempts at emancipation were.

But since brute force alone is never enough to quell popular aspiration, the Brahmins employed the gentler art of persuasion to keep at bay any feelings of resentment. Suddenly there was a religious revival with greater emphasis on pageantry, festivals, scripture recitals and charity, but with a difference: the harijans who were kept out of these activities in the past were the main targets now. Ingenious ways were devised to maintain a minimum distance while drawing them closer: they were allowed to enter the yard but not the temple and they could participate in all the ceremonies without touching any of the sacred objects. Songs and scriptures that glorified the innate equality of human beings were selected for every occasion. Kabir and Rahim jostled for pride of place with the *Ramcharitmanas*. Yet, at all times, social hierarchy was strictly maintained. One thing was made clear to everybody: true welfare depended on the continuation of this order.

Murari Pandit supported the movement wholeheartedly. Damodar was appalled at the way he used his sermons to educate rather than to subjugate. He even began a literacy programme for the adults and persuaded Chandra to talk to the village women about basic hygiene, childcare and healthy food habits. She also taught them needlework, knitting and the rudiments of reading and writing. To add to Damodar's chagrin, all the money for these projects was drawn from the temple fund. Heeriya and Ramdas were important allies of Murari, for their implicit faith and gratitude went a long way towards overcoming the natural suspicions of the rest of their community. The couple also served as role models for the other harijans. They were living proof that social uplift was possible with personal effort and a little cooperation from the higher castes.

Murari's dreams, in fact, were much bigger than Damodar could have imagined. He had planned to start a school exclusively for the dalits and had approached the state government for a grant. Naturally, they had agreed to provide funds, but on condition that Murari would donate some land and that the temple would have to bear a part of the cost. Murari was ecstatic. He informed Damodar that the four-acre field behind the temple used till now for the cultivation of bajra and mustard seed would be the site for this school, and that the seed money and a regular allowance for its maintenance would be taken from the temple fund.

This was the final straw for Damodar and a violent quarrel ensued. But Murari, not one to be intimidated or convinced otherwise, stayed his ground. In the end, Damodar thought up a plan that would kill two birds with one stone. He suggested that Murari take charge of their second temple in Vindhyachal and set up the school there. Damodar would treat this as a partition and would not interfere with Murari's plans. Under Murari's able stewardship, the new temple would become a centre for social revival and more people would benefit. Realizing that an independent charge would remove many difficulties and allow him to pursue his dreams unhampered, Murari decided to take up Damodar's offer. Besides, it would permit Chandra to participate more fully in his projects and help her to break out of her depression caused by her barrenness. Damodar's wife never lost an opportunity to remind her that sterility was a curse and that she was paying for Murari's follies

But when Murari and Chandra told their loyal followers about their plans, they had to face some tough questions. How could their Mai-Baap leave them in the lurch in this manner, they asked. In answer, Murari pointed to Shankar, Damodar's elder son, a good-looking, educated youth, and promised that he would carry on Murari's work. In any case, Ramdas and Heeriya would continue in their offices and keep Murari informed of the day-to-day developments.

Shankar, however, had other plans. Following his father's example, he had always believed that Murari Pandit's liberalism was inimical to their position. It did not occur to him that by befriending the harijans they could widen their power base and become true leaders, or that Murari had laid the foundation for such a possibility. His narrow parochialism could only visualize a 'we' and a 'they', not an 'us'. Soon after Murari left, Shankar set out to undo the changes that Murari had worked so hard to bring about in the last decade.

The pujas and festivals continued, but the dalits were no longer invited. If they were, they were not given any prasad. Even the flowers and offerings they brought were pointedly left outside in the yard. The temple no longer helped them to market their wares. However, this was not accepted as meekly by them as Shankar had expected. Angry people gathered around the temple, protesting loudly, and demanded that the temple, as much as it might belong to the Brahmins, was theirs as well. Ramdas and Heeriya led the protest. They also appealed to Murari for help. Murari came down the next day and tried to reason with Shankar, but the arrogant Shankar simply told him to mind his own business—the temple was out of his jurisdiction now; only Shankar's word mattered.

Defeated, Murari told Heeriya, Ramdas and the others that they would have to fight their own battles; nobody could help them if they couldn't find the strength within themselves to continue the effort.

This was easier said than done. The discipline and sustained effort that such resistance would require was difficult to find among a people who had lost the faith to make a bid for betterment. The whole affair would have died a natural death had it not been for Heeriya, who absolutely refused to see her dreams of a bright future collapse so easily. After some deliberation with Ramdas and her friends, she decided to draw the women of her community into her orbit. She visited them, called them to meetings, and explained to them that as mothers they had a duty to their children, born and unborn: their children must never be shackled as they themselves had been. The response was unexpectedly enthusiastic. Soon, the meetings held just beyond the panchvati became larger, more united and focused. In a few weeks, their path lay clear before them and they appealed to Damodar, gently to begin with and then more insistently, that the temple resume its role as the leader of social regeneration and the restrictions be done away with. Intimidated, Damodar succumbed to the pressure, and a semblance of goodwill was restored. But suspicion and resentment on both sides continued to vitiate the relationship.

Shankar was furious at the turn of events and was determined to break the back of this new movement. He identified Heeriya as its motive force and concluded that if she was removed from the scene, these determined and organized women would be as helpless as the proverbial flock of sheep. But a devious method would have to be thought of; direct attack would not only incur the wrath of the entire community, leading to magisterial intervention, but also bring Murari back as an implacable enemy. The thought began to plague him day and night.

Although Heeriya and Ramdas had been married for five years, they had no children. Normally, Ramdas would have taken a second wife, but his respect for Heeriya had precluded such a course of action. It was evident, however, that he longed for a son, and it broke Heeriya's heart that she could not grant him his desire. It had never occurred to her that Ramdas may be the sterile one and she blamed herself endlessly for her inadequacy till one evening, during a scripture reading session at the temple, she heard a story from the *Mahabharata*. When Vichitravirya, prince of Hastinapur, died without leaving any heirs to the throne, his worri d mother Satyavati turned to Bhishma for advice. Bhishma reminded her that the Shastras had sanctioned a course of action for just such a desperate situation——a Brahmin of high character could be called upon to provide the dynasty with an heir. Satyavati then sent Bhishma to the great sage Veda Vyasa, and Pandu, Dhritarashtra and Vidura were born to the queens Amba, Ambalika and a hand-maiden respectively. She realized suddenly that the man, and not necessarily the woman, could be the barren one. Her simple mind also registered the fact that one could step out of the marriage bond to have a child, provided a suitable father could be found. Shankar, always on the prowl and sneaking around Heeriya's room to find out what plans were afoot, heard her discussing the issue quite seriously with a friend, and his corrupt, scheming brain hit upon a ploy. He was not certain of success, but knew Heeriya enough to reason that it was worth a try.

One night while Ramdas was away in a neighbouring village, Heeriya awoke with a start as firm hands clasped over her mouth. It was Shankar. He explained that he had been attracted to her for a long time now and he knew how miserable she was without a child. Since he was a Brahmin, a child fathered by him should be acceptable just as it was in earlier times as she had heard in the reading of the scriptures. In any case, Ramdas need never know who the father was—at least he would be happy. Heeriya did not know that if she disagreed he would rape her anyway and use the incident to blackmail her into submission. She wanted so desperately to believe him that she did, and opened herself to him.

Ramdas's almost pathetic elation at the news of Heeriya's pregnancy three months later washed away the lingering doubts from her mind and she concentrated completely on her unborn child. The meetings with the other women became fewer, Heeriya was less vocal about her demands for her community and Shankar congratulated himself on the success of his strategy. He had enjoyed himself thoroughly and now the firebrand, indebted to him for life, had ceased to be a thorn in his side.

During the first few months of pregnancy, Heeriya remained completely absorbed in the creative process going on within her. She examined her body minutely for any outward changes and was elated when her belly began to show a new roundness and her breasts grew heavier. The midwife, a good friend, advised regular massages with warm mustard oil, good food and regular housework. In the seventh month, some of her friends got together to make laddus out of besan, ghee and sugar with dill, aniseed and basil and brought them over to Heeriya. They made her wear a new sari, lit a lamp and proceeded to feed her ceremonially. When the celebrations were over, one of Heeriya's closest allies told Heeriya that she and the others wanted to talk to her about something important. Heeriya admitted rather guiltily that she had had no contact with them for the last few months, but now that she was more accustomed to carrying her baby inside her she would resume her duties. Then the bitter truth began to emerge: the women had been forbidden to hold meetings. There had been quite a few cases of lynching and one or two women had disappeared from the village, particularly the more vocal ones. No one knew what had become of them. The lathials had become very active and closely scrutinized the people who came to the temple. The thin stream of charity from the temple fund was now being distributed among renegades and turncoats who found it materially beneficial to side with the Mishras and the Thakurs against their own community.

By the time the women left, the sun was setting. The slanting rays faded over the treetops and lengthening shadows crept across the panchvati into the temple yard. Heeriya, standing on her doorstep, stared into the distance as her friends made their way home. Chants from the *Ramcharitmanas* resounded in her mind: Ram, the great king, hugs Guhak, the untouchable, and calls him a friend. On another occasion, he partakes of the fruit that Sharbari, the low-caste woman, has tasted to ensure that they are sweet. Kabir's songs which say that it is the individual's identity as a human being is all-important, not the colour or creed. Murari and Chandra sacrificing their own peace for her people. Her marriage to Ramdas and their joint ventures. The exhilaration of effort and achievement. Then, her own needs taking precedence over all considerations leading ultimately to blindness and betrayal. Shankar could enter my body and still call himself a Brahmin, she thought. What gave him this superiority? How was he different from Ramdas? Slowly it dawned on her that it was not god who created, castes, men like Damodar and Shankar did . . . And her heart sank as she realized how they had used her to further their nefarious ends.

A wave of revulsion flooded her mind and body at the thought that she was carrying Shankar's child in her womb. She picked up the bhojali that Ramdas had left behind for her protection, ready to end her shame once and for all. Her only regret was that she had not used the dagger the night Shankar had entered her room. Then she lowered her upraised hand. Not like this, she thought. She could still make amends. She put away the dagger, calmed herself and managed to greet Ramdas with a semblance of normalcy when he returned.

From the next day, Heeriya resumed her trips to the homes of her co-workers. The meetings began again. A delegation of women demanded an audience with Damodar to inquire about the girls who had disappeared and the men who had been beaten to death. Taken completely by surprise, Damodar at first tried to browbeat them into submission. But when Heeriya appeared on the scene, flaunting her eight-month pregnant belly, he was cowed, for he was aware of the paternity of the child. Late at night, he called Shankar to his room. They conferred into the small hours of the morning but were unable to devise a satisfactory plan of action. Heeriya's aggressive attitude had turned the tables neatly on the Mishras and they realized that Shankar would have to leave the village if the truth became common knowledge. The child that was meant to be a boon was turning into a curse. Shankar tried to see Heeriya, but she openly turned her back on him. She had stopped Ramdas from making overnight visits anywhere, and her friends took turns to be with her constantly so that she was never alone in the room.

Towards the end of the ninth month, Heeriya went into labour. It was hard and painful. But Heeriya welcomed the pain. With every spasm she felt she was expiating a tiny fraction of her great sin. Not a cry escaped her lips and the midwife, wiping the sweat pouring from her face and body, was amazed at her fortitude. After a gruelling fight of four hours, the midwife announced joyfully, 'It's a boy!' She cut the umbilical cord, handed the baby to Gulabiya, who wrapped him in swaddling clothes, and helped Heeriya clean up. Then she placed two pillows behind Heeriya and helped her sit up, handing the baby to her. Ramdas entered the room beaming. 'Our child, Heeriya, after so many years of prayer,' he whispered to Heeriya, gazing in awe at the screaming baby in her arms.

But Heeriya could not hear him. In the tiny, shrivelled features of the baby she tried to trace Shankar's lustful face as he had loomed over her. But what of the other half—the earth that had nurtured the seed—her own flesh, her own blood? For a few agonizing moments she held the baby close. He snuggled to her, looking for the teat that would provide life. Heeriya could feel her breasts fill up with milk and every instinct in her cried out to guide the tiny mouth to the bursting nipple. Then her son opened his eyes and as she looked down at them she could see no innocence, no love, nothing but Shankar staring at her mockingly. She straightened her back and turned her head away, as her hands fastened around the child's throat . . .

Ramdas rushed to take the baby from her. There were no cries, no tears, only a little head lolling to one side, like a broken doll. The midwife screamed, just one word into the silence like a single pebble hitting the surface of a vast blue lake: Why? The stillness trembled, the air vibrated, as the explanation dropped, word by word, factual, precise, completely unemotional, from Heeriya's lips. Then she rose, took the baby from Ramdas, and said, 'I will take the son to his father. You can come with me if you wish to.' Without faltering, she carried the baby across the panchvati, and laid him at Shankar's feet. Word travelled like lightning, and by the time Damodar entered the scene to unearth the cause of the furore, the lathials close behind, the temple's 'sanctity' had been defiled completely for it was full of harijans.

In the mayhem that followed, in which Shankar was killed and his father and brother maimed for life, no one noticed Heeriya slipping away. Her determined steps took her straight to the river that sustained life in this arid land. She stepped into the water. It lapped around her ankles, then rose to her knees and up her thighs till it encircled her waist like a lover, then caressed her breasts like her child might have. She did not stop when the water entered her nose and mouth, sucking out the life-giving air, and closed over her head. A minute or two later there was scarcely a ripple disturbing its surface. The river had regained its serenity.

1962

The Miracle

BARODA IN MAHARASHTRA WAS ONE PRINCELY STATE THAT HAD combined the conveniences of modernization with a significant cultural revival under British rule. One of the five famous ruling families of this province, the Gae7kwads, had paid great attention to education, agriculture and public welfare in a bid to beat the British at their own game. After independence India's new leaders realized the foolishness of maintaining enclaves of individual power within a country that was struggling to achieve unity and the princely states were brought under the Indian administrative system. The royal families, however, retained their palaces, titles, personal wealth and some of the properties. The Gaekwads gave up their famous Lal Bagh palace so that the premises could be utilized for a much-needed railway staff college. Another magnificent edifice belonging to them, the Makarapura Palace, was made into a museum. The family, however, continued to play a prominent role in the social circles. The dowager queen, Savita Devi, led a group of ladies in valuable social work and she was ably assisted in this enterprise by the present queen, her daughter-in-law, who hailed from the state of Jodhpur in Rajasthan. People who met the queen swore that the diamonds she wore could not be real—so large, lustrous and magnificent were these jewels!

Although the Gaekwads were Hindus, the Christian, Muslim and Jain communities had coexisted peacefully in their state while they were the rulers. In the late 1950s, however, the situation changed. Hindu fundamentalists steadily took over professional circuits, municipal positions, police circles and business interests. Located close to Bombay, the city that was fast emerging as the business centre of independent India, Baroda was beginning to see itself as a player in the national power game. Land prices soared, and greedy eyes were cast at properties held by non-Hindu communities.

One of the last bastions of liberalism was the Baroda University and the schools and colleges within its purview. In appreciation of the valuable work done by missionary schools in India, the authorities had so far cooperated with them in every way. But the new breed of politicians who used their religiosity as a cloak for their personal ambitions and nefarious activities, began to spread ugly rumours about compulsory Bible classes, forced conversions and 'rice' Christians. Some students were withdrawn from the schools, but the elite of Baroda continued to send their girls to the Convent of Jesus and Mary. The support of these powerful patrons kept the school free of spatial and intellectual encroachment.

The sprawling four-acre compound of the convent in the heart of the city was an oasis of greenery and peace. Of the three large buildings, two housed classrooms, laboratories and studios, while the third served as the living quarters for the nuns and the orphan girls who had found refuge there. The school was managed by two American nuns, Mother Luke and Mother Roland, who did their best to enliven the staid syllabi prescribed by the University of Cambridge and the Bombay Matriculation Board. They encouraged the students to think for themselves and organized lively debates on varied subjects so every student got a chance to speak her mind. A dynamic woman characterized by a robust realism and a wonderful sense of humour, Mother Roland's classes on ethics and English literature were particularly unforgettable. She maintained, unequivocally, that ethics and ethos were inseparable; preaching without practising constituted the greatest sin. The students, who found her working indefatigably between bouts of malaria that left her pale and weak but unshaken in her resolve, learnt to appreciate that she was teaching them by example rather than by precept.

Having worked in many troubled areas in Africa and Latin America before coming to India, Mother Luke was familiar with the political patterns of countries attaining freedom from foreign rule—the greed, the dishonesty, the power games—and in her own quiet and efficient way, she had taken precautions to protect her school against danger. One of these was an arrangement with Hans Doring, whose daughters also studied in the school, to call the school every evening to check if everything was all right. He had instructions that in the event of failing to make a connection, he should come down immediately to the school to ensure that everyone was safe.

While it was popular knowledge that Hans, a talented sculptor, and his Jewish wife, Mae, had escaped by the skin of their teeth from a concentration camp during the Second World War, very few people knew that Hans had been in the police force in Prussia before he married Mae. His revolver was always kept under his pillow when he slept; experience had taught him to depend on himself and his gun at all times. Hans was also a naturalist of some repute and often spent entire afternoons hunting for specimens in the jungles on the outskirts of the city. On one such occasion he was bitten on his right wrist by a krait. Without wasting a moment, Hans had made a tourniquet out of his handkerchief, just below the elbow, with the help of his hands and teeth, and ridden six miles to his doctor on his trusty bicycle, steering with his left hand and turning the right arm constantly in a circle from the shoulder so that the centrifugal motion would keep the poison away from his heart and brain. He collapsed only after he had told the doctor exactly how to administer the serum. His family and friends found out about the incident many months later from the doctor, who could not stop talking about Hans's courage and presence of mind.

One summer, before the school was to close for the vacations, the nuns organized a Parliament of Religions and invited guest speakers to exchange their views and experiences with the senior girls. Mr Mukerji, principal of the railway staff college and a Brahmin, opened the debate with a paper titled 'My Father's house has many mansions'. With copious references to the Gita, Torah, Bible and Koran, he stressed the commonality of religions, their shared principles and values, their identical objectives. He emphasized that Hinduism was a philosophy to be lived by rather than just a collection of scriptures meant to be recited at pujas and ceremonies. Mr Sayeed, an officer in the Indian Administrative Service and a Muslim, who knew the Gita as well as he knew the Koran, traced the common roots of Islam, Christianity and Judaism. He also believed that Hinduism, older than the other three religions, had influenced them. In their own presentations the nuns stressed practical Christianity—community welfare, promotion of education and enlightenment. They expressed their belief in fostering both personal and social consciousness, while keeping alive the spiritual yearning that is inherent in every human being.

The most moving speech was by Mae Doring, Hans's wife. 'I have seen my own people turn against me because of religious differences,' she said. 'It is difficult for me to describe the ignominy of being a Jew not only in

Germany but in the rest of Europe as well, and of having the Star of David pinned inexorably on your sleeve. If it had not been for Hans, who is by the way a Lutheran Christian, my family and I would have perished in the flames of the Holocaust. I know of no life beyond this one and no God apart from man. Man is God, man is Devil, and the cosmic game is played out on the battlefield of these forces.'

The event sent the reputation of the school soaring to new heights. The education department, not wishing to lose out on the limelight, declared that the school deserved a more substantial grant, and an Inspector of Schools appeared one morning to ascertain whether the school met the criteria laid down by the department. A minute inspection of the buildings, playground, basic facilities and the credentials of teachers proved that these were quite impeccable. The school's kitchens were models of hygiene, the orphanage was airy, spacious and comfortable, the fine library, well-equipped laboratories and various teaching aids pointed to wise and vigilant management. The Inspector found it strange that most of the staff was non-Christian and noted that educational qualifications and experience counted more than religious conformity when it came to the appointments made by the nuns who ran the school. The only stumbling blocks were the two American nuns themselves who were strangely loath to speak of their past lives and their own qualifications.

The Inspector was convinced he had found the Achilles' heel in this armour of perfection, and demanded in a stentorian tone to see some proof of their qualifications. The nuns disappeared into their living quarters like two guilty schoolgirls and emerged with some dusty, dog-eared files. The contents of the files nearly gave the Inspector a heart attack. Mother Luke had a degree in Divinity from Cambridge, a master's degree in English literature from Stanford and the highest postgraduate qualification in teaching. Impressive enough. Mother Roland hailed from one of the oldest landowning families of Rhode Island, whose lineage could be traced back to the French aristocracy. She spoke four languages, read Latin, had a Ph.D. in Classics from Browns and a Ph.D. in biology from Johns Hopkins. Very quietly, she told the Inspector that her three brothers always used their own airplanes to travel and that she was a champion swimmer. In fact, her home in Rhode Island had an Olympic-sized swimming pool. Of her three sisters, two had chosen to become nuns—not because they lacked anything, but because they had too much. She had come to India because she was fascinated by its ancient culture and felt privileged to work in the country. She also begged him not to disclose the details of her life to anyone.

The Inspector made hasty promises to keep the information to himself, but within a few days the local newspaper carried a story about the school and 'the brilliant team that managed it'. This drew much attention to the school and many a doubting Thomas rushed to admit his daughter to this 'premier institution', much to the amusement of the nuns.

The school's orphanage housed about forty girls of mixed origin. Some had been here practically since their birth and had completely adopted the ethos of the school. They studied with the day scholars and most of them had planned their careers and worked steadfastly towards their goals. A few others had joined the orphanage in their early childhood and had fallen into the prevailing pattern. But there was a group of six girls who had been 'sent' to the school by municipal authorities for rehabilitation, social and moral. These children found it very difficult to accept the strict discipline they had to maintain: the work and study schedules were much too demanding and the moral standards utterly uncompromising. They were in their teens and the world outside the convent walls held many attractions for them. Mother Roland, who had picked up the native languages—Gujarati and Marathi—quite easily, had no problems communicating with them and tried to spend as much time as possible interacting with them. She made it a point to keep 'right' and 'wrong' totally out of the way and tried to lure them away from their earlier way of life by painting the picture of a secure and worthwhile future for each of them. After many years of effort, she seemed to be making some headway and was happy with the progress that most of the girls had made. The only person on whom Mother Roland's magic did not work at all was Maria, a girl as strange in nature as she was in appearance.

Maria was obviously of mixed parentage, for she combined a dark complexion with golden hair and startling blue eyes. Tall and well built, with curved, sensuous lips and a slightly beaked nose, she was a striking, if a rather repelling, figure. It is correct to say, perhaps, that though she seemed considerably repulsive at first sight first, closer scrutiny revealed her charms. Maria was an intelligent girl and schoolwork held no terrors for her. She had climbed steadily up the academic ladder in the seven years that she had been in the school and was now one of the middling students in the tenth grade. The school authorities hoped that after passing her matriculation she would carry on with her education and eventually train to be a nurse.

Outward conformity had, however, not touched Maria's soul in any way. Maria could never forgive her mother for deserting her and thus compelling her to come to the convent. She hazily remembered her carefree days with her mother—the tawdry world of easy come, easy go, when money was plentiful. On lean days she depended on her cunning and guile to earn enough for a good meal. Her mother's friends, particularly the men, sometimes gave her a rupee or two in passing. There was no school, no routine and no discipline to worry about. She spent all her time with the children in her neighbourhood, particularly with a boy named Rudy who was beginning to hint at mysterious, unknown and forbidden pleasures. Then her mother disappeared. A neighbour informed Maria that her mother had gone off to Bombay with a friend who had not wanted Maria to accompany them. Then she had been told to pack her belongings and was deposited at the nearby police station. From there, bedraggled and hungry, she had been led to the convent. She had hated its clean, antiseptic atmosphere from the very first moment and couldn't wait to get back to her own world. If anyone attempted to probe, Maria quickly sought refuge in inscrutability. She had a trick of closing her eyes without dropping the lids, like a cat, so that the person who was speaking to her would be uncomfortably aware that she was miles away, immersed in her thoughts. Her teachers and peers were wary of her and most of the girls in the orphanage steered clear of any interaction with her. The only person who realized that her apparent indifference was a façade for the deep hurt and rage against life that smouldered within her was Mother Roland and she continued relentlessly to attack this invisible barrier. She was confident that some day her love for Maria would triumph, that Maria would ultimately confide in her of her own accord.

But no one in the convent knew about Rudy, Maria's special friend from her childhood days. His influence on her was immense, her attraction to him overwhelming. Time after time she had managed to evade the school's strict security to maintain contact with him. A strapping youth of twenty, Rudy belonged to a group of well-known criminals who terrorized the neighbourhood. Rudy's boss, Kishen, was only thirty years old, but already immensely powerful owing to his intelligence and foresight. Starting out as a criminal at a very young age, he had built up strong connections with the politicians and the police. Safe in the knowledge that no one could touch them, his group had grown brazen and engaged in all kinds of nefarious activities. Kishen was well aware of Rudy's liaison with Maria, and therefore the convent. Rudy had told him how desperate Maria was to get away from the convent and that some day Kishen would have to help him get her out. Kishen, however, had a different plan clearly worked out in his head. He would use this opportunity to kill three birds with one stone: to draw more girls from the orphanage into his orbit, to reward Rudy for his loyal service by getting Maria out of the convent and, most importantly, to discredit the convent in the process. This would keep the politicians happy and assure their continued patronage. He advised Rudy to hold his horses and to tell Maria to work on the other girls so that they too would want to leave the convent with Maria when the time came.

Impatient to get away from the convent to a world which she knew would be fraught with dangers and deprivation but still held for her the promise of total freedom and fulfilment, Maria got to work immediately. To her surprise and satisfaction she found it quite easy to convince the others of the futility of education. The lure of money, freedom and flesh was quite irresistible to the girls who had seen little of the humane side of life and they wanted to leave the convent immediately.

Christmas was a joyous time at the convent—a time for carol singing, special services, nativity plays, dramatic productions and fêtes. But the two weeks between Christmas and Epiphany was a period of quiet meditation and retreat. With the school closed for the rest of winter, students, teachers and domestic help went home for the holidays, while the nuns and the girls in the orphanage managed with a skeleton staff. The trusted darwan Bhola had gone to his village for a week and left his son Ramu to officiate. Mother Roland utilized this period to work with the examinees from the orphanage, for whom English was the main stumbling block.

Maria told Rudy that this was the time to strike: the school was unprotected; they would have only the two nuns and a few dissenting girls to contend with; and since the local police station was in Kishen's pay there was no fear of any interference from that quarter.

It was the first week of January. The bitter cold had confined most people to their homes. Traffic was light and pedestrians few and far between. When Kishen and Rudy arrived at the convent with two henchmen in tow, the place wore a deserted look. Ramu was in the little gatehouse warming his hands over a small fire. It took them a couple of seconds to knock him out cold and cut the telephone lines. They then proceeded towards the orphanage, confident that the girls would be in the study hall and the nuns busy with evening prayers. It would be a simple matter to walk out with the five girls they had targeted. They anticipated no resistance, but were armed with knives and guns to deal with opposition if required.

Today, however, was the feast of Epiphany, celebrating the journey made by the three wise men to pay homage to a humble child lying in a manger. A special evening service had been organized with hymns and prayers. The sound of a choir singing clearly indicated that the entire population was in the chapel. Light streamed out from the windows and made patterns on the cold, dark ground, permitting the men to take a good look. Mother Luke was conducting the service along with another nun. Mother Roland was at the piano, leading the singing. The girls knelt in the pews and the singers stood around the piano.

Abide with me, amid the encircling gloom.
The night is dark and I am far from home ...

The clear voices rang out like a chime of bells and Kishen found unaccustomed doubts assailing him. Suddenly he felt unnerved by strange misgivings; yet he didn't know why, since he could anticipate no dangerous obstacles. 'Not tonight,' he said slowly. 'We'll come back later.' But Rudy and the other two men who had been gearing up for some action with one drink after another would listen to nobody. He strode forward and knocked on the door. The door opened and the men rushed in before it could be closed again. Kishen, who followed them in unwillingly, spoke up. 'We will not hurt you. We have only come to take our friends. Let them go, and we will leave.'

Rudy called out to Maria, who urged her friends to move forward with her. Swiftly, Mother Roland blocked their way without a word.

'I told you, not tonight,' Kishen whispered urgently in Rudy's ear, trying to drag him away by the arm. 'We don't want an ugly incident on our hands.'

But Rudy was too far gone to care. One of the men uttered a filthy oath and said, 'Let's kick this bitch out of the way!' Another reached for her habit.

Mother Roland stood unflinching as the hand closed over her wimple, pulling at it and then, her eyes widened.

Standing behind Kishen was Hans Doring, the revolver
in his hand pointing straight at Kishen's back.

In the black
melting pot
the colours
in a mad
medley spun
till all was
one—the light
that filled the
nave and altar
merged with the radiance that glowed on the cross
where Christ drooped under the crown of thorns,
vinegar lacerating his sweet lips, rusty nails drawing blood
from hand and foot
and breast;
then flowed
again to reach
and engulf
the woman
unflinching,
unfeeling of
barbaric hands
that clutched
and pawed
till the blood

flowed from
her foot
and hands
and breast
till the two
were one——
the Maker
or the made?

The gun fell from Hans's nerveless hand and he dropped to his knees. The three intoxicated men looked as though they'd seen a ghost. The man clutching at the wimple withdrew as if stung by a scorpion, his face contorted with pain. Rudy, his face ashen, turned to Kishen and said, 'Let's get the hell out of here!' Heads lowered they didn't stop running till they reached their den.

When Hans regained his composure, Mother Roland was trying to calm a hysterical, sobbing Maria and Mother Luke was speaking quietly to the other girls. Then they made a pact, all of them, that the affairs of the night would remain within the walls of the chapel and never be discussed again. By the time Ramu regained consciousness and rushed to the chapel, Hans had left and the girls were at supper. Mother Luke told Ramu that there had been intruders but Hans had turned up at the nick of time, alerted when no one answered his routine evening phone call; Ramu must have knocked his head on the ledge and passed out for a few minutes, she explained to the anxious man.

Hans did not tell anybody about his experience that night, not even Mae. When his daughters asked him why he had rushed to their school, he said it was because he had failed to make a telephone connection but when he reached there he had found everybody at prayer and had returned without speaking to anyone. But there was never a moment in his life after that when he did not think about what he had witnessed in the church that night, and wonder whether it had been a miracle or just an illusion.

1968

The Quilt

HER EARLIEST MEMORIES ARE THOSE OF HER MOTHER STANDING with her head lowered and trembling from head to toe, while her father endlessly berates her. As he speaks, the sound of his own voice somehow intensifies his sense of injury at some imagined infringement of his authority. Gradually, it gains in pitch and volume and expletives flow out unhindered till his temper reaches such a pitch that he lashes out with the first object he can lay his hands on. The wooden slipper scrapes her mother's temple and draws blood as she falls to the ground in a heap. The child cowers in a corner, wishing she were invisible, and does not approach her mother till the man has left the room. Then, with her small and frail hands, she caresses her mother's cheeks as tears stream silently down her pallid face.

They are part of a large joint family, like a banyan tree reaching out to anchor its buttress roots in the ground and consume more territory. The roots are gnarled but strong; the leaves are large, green and shiny; the berries are poison-red. The tree itself is unaware that its main bole is termite ridden and rotting from within. The green of its leaves is born out of envy, the red of the berries out of rage.

Janardan, the man who had put the family on the social map at the turn of the century, had been a man of vision. A Brahmin himself, he had realized that the social order could survive only if its base was strengthened. He had thus thrown himself into the land reform movement and worked tirelessly at bettering the lot of the agricultural labourers who were entirely at the mercy of rapacious landlords. The labourers called him 'Dadaji' and loved him like a father and the landlords hated him in equal measure.

Janardan's son, the patriarch of this family, as shrewd as he was unscrupulous, was a clever lawyer and had built up their present property mainly by escheat. Many of his clients had lost hearth and home to fuel the fires of his avarice. He had three sons by his wife and a parallel family through his concubine, for whom he had provided lavishly. He made no secret of his preference and his legitimate children had grown up in the shadow of their father's mistress and her son.

The present head of the family, Narayan, and his two younger brothers, Kashinath and Baldeo, have neither the spirit of their grandfather nor the ability of their father. They are small men striving for stature, which constantly eludes them. The fact that their stepbrother, Santosh, has trained in law and is on his way to becoming a political leader does not help. The neighbours miss no opportunity to make humiliating references to their inadequacy and the brothers look to each other for support and absolution.

Narayan and Kashinath have married and only the latter has a son, Ramesh, which has endowed him with some prestige within and without the family. Narayan has one daughter, Rama, but after that his wife has been unable to conceive. Narayan blames her entirely for this and believes that it legitimizes his onslaughts on her. Unfortunately, his wife thinks the same. Her meek acceptance of the daily bouts of verbal and physical assault only eggs him on to further brutality. Elated at the smallness of his two elder stepbrothers, Santosh takes a perverse pleasure in ruining Baldeo completely. He has introduced the fifteen-year-old to cigarettes and alcohol and lavishes money on him so he can indulge in these habits and much worse.

By a strange quirk of fate, little Rama seems to have inherited the brains of her grandfather, and at ten years displays the spirit that had been Janardan's alone. The headmaster of the local school which she attends thinks very highly of her. Whenever he bumps into Narayan at the market or on the street, he begs him to send Rama to the better-equipped government school. 'Kashinath has sent his idiot son to that expensive missionary school,' he pleads with Narayan. 'Rama is far, far cleverer, you know.' At first, Narayan will hear none of it. 'She's only a girl. What use will all this learning be to her? If she is not barren like her mother and can bear her husband sons, that will be enough for me,' he says gruffly.

But the headmaster is a persistent, annoying man, and Narayan has to give in eventually. Rama joins the government school and is ranked at the top of her class in no time. She also makes many friends and begins to realize that other people live a lot differently from her family. Now, when her father goes too far and starts beating her mother, she does not retreat into her shell and watch silently but actually tries to protest. Her outbursts have earned her some blows but not deterred her. In fact, Narayan now avoids confronting his wife in her presence.

Partially released from the pressures of seeing her mother suffer, spending time at school with happy, young people and reading books for pleasure, Rama flowers into an attractive, happy teenager. Her sharp face, pinched and insignificant before, begins to take on a new beauty. Her small waist, neat hands and feet, and thick, dark coil of hair make people forget that she is dark—a cardinal sin in Brahmin households. Her bewitching smile, rare and often confined to the corner of her chiselled lips, is an uncomfortable reminder to her father and his brothers that her dark eyes see and comprehend a great deal that lies below the surface and beyond the obvious.

One day Rama goes to her father with a request that is as strange as it is novel: she wants her father to become a member of the public library in their town so she can have access to the books in the children's section. Narayan remonstrates with his daughter, saying that the books are in English and would be of little use to her. 'But I'm learning English in school, Baba,' Rama argues, 'and my teacher told me that if I read more books, I will speak English even better.' Her persistence compels her father to comply, albeit reluctantly.

The librarian, Mr Sullivan, is taken aback by the girl's insatiable appetite for knowledge and instinctive love of all things new. He takes charge of her reading and guides her towards the books that will appeal to her. Within a year she has graduated from *Aesop's Fables* to Lamb's *Tales From Shakespeare*, *Alice inWonderland* and Tennyson's poems. One day Mr Sullivan introduces her to a senior teacher of English at the missionary school, Miss Rutherford, who has seen her visit the library every evening and has asked the librarian about her. This time, it is Miss Rutherford who approaches Narayan and insists that he send Rama to her school. After much debate and discussion he gives in, though with poor grace. Here too Rama shines among her classmates as her aptitude for mathematics and science is no less phenomenal than her linguistic abilities. All the teachers are sure she will bring distinction to their school in the public examinations, and they unite in their efforts to promote her education.

Narayan is bewildered by his daughter's progress. On the one hand he feels that it is not 'right' to give her such opportunities; she is after all just a girl. On the other hand, he cannot help being proud of her achievements. In any case, he feels, it is too late to withdraw his support and prevent her progress. The rest of the family, however, is not ready to accept this change so meekly. The most vocal are Kashinath, for Ramesh is repeating the year in class six yet again, and Baldeo, who is at the point of being expelled from school. They mount a joint attack on Narayan, saying that his selfish decisions have brought shame on the family and that Rama's 'character' is a source of embarrassment to them. The memsahibs are encouraging her to play games, to sing, to participate in the school drama. Surely, no girl from a decent home does these things. Narayan must withdraw her from school and insist that she concentrate on cleaning the house, cooking for the family and sewing. After all, isn't it time they thought about getting her married? But Narayan, a small, resentful man, who is loath to give up the opportunity to feel proud of his daughter's success, opposes each argument. Rama is only twelve, he says, she can continue to study for another year or two at least. After that, he will think of looking for a groom for her. Thwarted, they turn to Rama's mother, Shobha, threatening her with dire consequences to Rama's well-being if she does not get Narayan to change his mind. Painfully aware of what these men are capable of, Shobha pleads desperately with father and daughter. When no amount of reasoning works, she resorts to tears, beating her chest and crying that if anything untoward happens to her daughter, Narayan will be cursed for not preventing it. Narayan remains unmoved, but Rama sits down by her wreck of a mother and promises quietly to pay more attention to household chores.

And so Rama learns how to stitch a quilt. Pieces of old cloth are stitched together in layers to the required thickness. This is covered with new cloth and stitches are run all along the quilt, vertically and horizontally, so that the layers are fixed firmly in place. Then comes the most interesting part—the entire surface is divided into two-inch squares which have to be filled in with embroidery. As Rama stares at the squares wondering which flower to embroider, a brilliant idea strikes her: the squares will record the events of her life but in code, so that no one will recognize them for what they really are.

The first square contains a nest. The second a family of birds. The third contains a little lame bird. In the fourth, the bird is hopping around, trying its wings, but a chain attached to its foot keeps it firmly tied to the nest. The bird flies to various places represented in the subsequent squares, but inevitably returns as the chain has a remarkably strong hold.

Meanwhile, Baldeo has been rusticated from his school and the missionary school Ramesh used to attend has requested his withdrawal for he has failed two years in succession. Ramesh convinces his father that Rama is somehow responsible for his failure. It is she who has turned all the teachers against him. Unless she leaves the school, he will never improve. But Kashinath can do little more than speak to Narayan again, and Ramesh turns to Baldeo for a remedy . . .

Two snakes have appeared on the quilt, one red, the other yellow. They have dark, malevolent eyes, and work their way surreptitiously from one square to the next. They climb the tree on which the nest is perched and make a home for themselves in a hollow in the tree, next to the nest. The little bird is wary and has found herself a friend—a bigger, brown bird who is with her all the time. But the snakes are always there too, keeping a close watch on them. Then, the friend falls ill. The little bird is all alone in her nest when the snakes slither into it. One of them mounts her and enters her little body as the other keeps watch. They take turns at ravaging her, then, satisfied, they slither away. The bird, more lame now than ever before, flutters around, dragging her broken wings. The scenes turn chaotic. The colours are violent and garish, the images strange and bizarre. But the snakes are omnipresent. They change colour and stance, appearing more ferocious than before. They chase the bird relentlessly and violate her again and again. There is no sequence now of the images on the quilt, no clarity, no recognizable form;

just a flood of red, spreading from square to square like rapidly seeping blood.

Shobha has noticed of late that her daughter is undergoing a strange transformation. It seems to Shobha that she is regressing, going back to where she was three years ago. She seems to have no confidence in herself, is reluctant to go to the market and even to school, and she clings to Shobha, sleeps with her, follows her everywhere, but does not say anything. When her friends come to call her to play with them, she tells them she is busy with housework and if she sits alone for even five minutes, tears course down her cheeks without her knowledge. Then, one day, Shobha finds the quilt, tucked under the pillow so carefully that no one would even know it's there. Her first impulse is to scold Rama for not showing her the wonderful embroidery. But as she scrutinizes the images, her eyes suddenly fall on the scene of the two snakes attacking the bird. Slowly her mind pieces together the sequence of events just as the quilt has done, and finally when she comes upon the red flood that drowns out every other colour, a terrible fear grips her heart.

Yet, she does nothing, for there is nothing she can do. She knows very well that the men will go scot-free, and the opprobrium will be all Rama's and hers. Besides, how will Narayan react? He will without doubt blame her for allowing Rama to step off the beaten track.

Shobha, eternally passive, cannot answer this call to action. In her desperation, she even tries to explain to Rama that her uncle and cousin 'love' her and this is their way of demonstrating it. Rama turns away from the inane excuses. Her sense of loss and alienation is complete, and she clings to the quilt as though it is her only lifeline. Her beloved books gather dust, her studies are forgotten. The designs on the quilt are no longer representational. The recurrent motif is a series of concentric rings ending in a back dot that gives a sense of endless darkness.

When Narayan asks Shobha why Rama is not attending school, she tells him that Rama has problems of a 'feminine' nature and needs to rest. Narayan accepts this explanation and does not probe further. The school, however, is less easy to appease, especially Miss Rutherford, who insists that she will visit Rama to see if there's anything she can do. Narayan hurriedly assures her that Rama will start attending school as soon as she is better. Back home, he confronts Shobha and demands an explanation: what is it precisely that is wrong with his daughter? Should Rama see a doctor?

After some prevarication, Shobha takes him to Rama's room. Hair unkempt, skin pallid, eyes glassy with unshed tears, Rama is lying in the foetal position, facing the wall, clutching the quilt to her chest. The shock Narayan gets at seeing his bright, sprightly daughter in this state weakens his resolve of facing the problem with his usual tactic—anger. He has always taken problems as a personal affront and reacted to them by launching a counteroffensive. For the first time he sees his wife and daughter not through the haze of egotism but as they are in reality—two defeated creatures on the brink of an abyss. He realizes, as he's never done before, that Rama is his only child, his tenuous claim to immortality, and he is afraid.

With unaccustomed gentleness, he sits on the bed, places his hand on Rama's head and asks whether she is in pain. The facile question overwhelms Rama, her furious attempt at self-control fails and a wild flood of tears mingles with the garbled torrent of words that have been waiting to escape her tortured lips. When it is over, Narayan sits uncomprehendingly for a few minutes. Then he gets up and withdraws to his room without a word. He does not have the spiritual resource to deal with the immensity of the situation.

That night, mother and daughter make a suicide pact. Their house is not too far from the railway tracks. The mail train that passes every morning at three will put them out of their misery. Yet, a question haunts Rama. Why must she pay the price for a sin that Ramesh and Baldeo have committed? Why will they get an opportunity to evade justice while she suffers? She lies in the dark, dry-eyed and seething with rage, not just at her tormentors, but at herself. Is she so weak that she will end it all without a fight? Finally, she gets up, creeps out of the room, lights a lamp and begins to work furiously on her quilt ...

The lame bird emerges from the flood of red. She hops a step or two, looks around and spies a mongoose. Ah! The killer of snakes! Dragging its broken wings, the little bird hops towards the mongoose. She is afraid, but determined.

She places the quilt on the empty pillow beside her mother's along with a letter addressed to her parents. Then she slips out of the house, walks four miles in the darkness, and knocks on Miss Rutherford's door.

When Shobha wakes up it's been a while since the mail train has passed. Turning to her side to wake Rama up, she finds the letter instead. By the time Narayan wakes up to his wife's screams as she beats furiously on his door and the other family members emerge to find out what all the commotion is about, half the town is at their doorstep. The whole sordid story is now common knowledge. Kashinath watches helplessly as Baldeo and Ramesh are taken away by the police. Santosh is nowhere to be found, and Mr Khanna, the magistrate, informs everybody in clear terms that the rape of a minor girl is a grave offence and the fact that an uncle and a cousin are the perpetrators will only make matters worse for the 'criminals'.

Rama goes back to school and continues to excel in all that she does. But within her there is a void, an emptiness that nothing can fill. It is as though her soul has been torn out, leaving her with an unclean body and a sterile mind. There are social pressures too that endorse this feeling. Kashinath insists that a wall be built to divide the house and grounds, so that Narayan and his family are completely isolated. A whispering campaign hints that the boys are more sinned against than sinning, that Rama had actually encouraged them in their advances. Neighbours tell their daughters not to play with Rama and she has no friends left in her locality. Even at school, the girls keep her company only because of Miss Rutherford. On her way to and from school several boys make indecent advances, saying that she should share her 'experience' with them and people point her out as 'the girl who was raped'.

Slowly a shell of loneliness begins to form around Rama and she retreats into it for protection. The quilt reappears and the squares begin to fill ...

The mongoose kills the two snakes and sets the bird free, but the bird is not able to fly. Out of the bellies of the dead snakes, a hundred snakes appear in a hundred different colours. They chase the bird all day, relentlessly. At the end of the road is a flowering tree which the bird desperately tries to reach knowing that safety lies on its leafy branches, but she's always just too far away from it.

Gradually Rama becomes obsessed with her alienation. She cringes away from all social contact and becomes paranoid about any gesture of affection, mistaking kindness for pity and reacting to people with unnecessary vehemence. Like a sapling in its prime struck by lightning, she withers physically and spiritually. *The flowering tree begins to drop its leaves and flowers, one by one, by one* ... The tremendous disturbance in her mind breaks out in the form of a violent eczema that threatens to ruin the contours of her face and spreads steadily down her throat. Her parents can no longer persuade her to go to school and even the quilt is abandoned.

Strangely enough, it is Narayan who takes the first step in the right direction. His job as a clerk in a small company is not a transferable one but he makes an appeal on compassionate grounds. Fortunately, his wish is granted within a month. They lock up their portion of the house, dismiss the servants and inform the school. On a cold and misty morning Narayan, Parvati and Rama wait on the railway platform with a few trunks and bags. The only people who come to see them off are Mr Sullivan, Miss Rutherford and a lone colleague of Narayan's. The last sound they hear as the train moves out of the station and three waving hands dissolve in the mist is of a dog yelping and whining as if in great pain. They sit in the compartment, dry-eyed and rigid, realizing perhaps for the first time that they have crossed the point of no return, that they are going into exile for the rest of their lives.

The train picks up speed and as the sun mounting higher in the sky breaks through the mist the landscape begins to change, and Narayan and Shobha are immediately transported into a new life, a new beginning. For the first time, Shobha will have her own home, and Narayan a job where nobody knows of his antecedents. But Rama's reaction is one of pure, burning rage at the injustice of it all: that she who had suffered should pay such a hideous price while her violators have escaped with a light sentence, that her parents, whatever their weaknesses, should be compelled to leave hearth and home in such ignominy. Her anger burns in her heart without a tremor, like a flame in a draughtless room, and intensifies as the train moves further and further away from the place she once called home.

Poona, where they are to set up their new home, is very different from their hometown. Being a cosmopolitan university town, its people are educated, liberal and forward-thinking. The bai, who works part-time for Shobha, treats her as an equal and a friendship of sorts develops between the two. The neighbours too seek Shobha out, and invite her for tea and conversation. Shobha, afraid of what Narayan's reaction will be, is very timid to begin with, but is amazed to find him much more relaxed as well. She cannot believe her ears when he tells her to go to the market for groceries, meet her neighbours and make friends. Free of the pressures of his family, Narayan too is able to concentrate on his work and is quite amazed at his own capabilities.

For Rama, though, things are not so simple; not because people are unkind, but because she no longer knows what it is like to trust another human being, to take people at face value. She misinterprets overtures of friendship from classmates and neighbours and attention from teachers as manifestations of pity. She takes no one into confidence and, consumed by anger, incarcerates herself in a torture chamber of self-flagellation. The eczema gets worse, travels down her throat and spreads across her breasts to her nipples. The quilt, which she now locks in her cupboard, is the silent recipient of her agony.

The lame bird stands inside a ring of fire that she cannot escape. Scorpions, maggots, beetles and strange, lizard-like creatures creep out of the fire and inch their way towards the bird. Cornered and desperate, the bird plunges into the fire to emerge scorched and barely alive but keeps running in search of shelter. The burn marks on her body are remarkably like the eczema that greets Rama in the mirror every morning. In pain, but imagining herself safe the bird rests under a bush, exhausted. And then . . . the sores on her body open one by one and the scorpions, maggots, beetles and lizard-like creatures slither out of them, covered in blood.

The doctor, who is treating Rama for her eczema, tells Narayan that it is merely a psychosomatic manifestation of her deep mental scars. He suggests a psychiatrist, but Rama will have none of it. She has been probed enough and will not permit further invasion. She continues to attend her classes and completes her board examinations. Her results though are not as spectacular as Miss Rutherford had once expected them to be.

College is a source of further trauma for Rama because it is coeducational. The easy camaraderie that exists between the girls and the boys horrifies her, but it also fills her with envy. She thinks she is the only one singled out by fate for punishment and her resentment at all the injustice she's had to face flares anew. Other than in the class or the library, she avoids any contact with her fellow students. In between classes she strictly avoids the cafeteria, closing her ears to the shrieks of laughter and the sounds of lighthearted banter that emanate from there, and walks to the edge of the campus where a gnarled, old fig tree provides shelter. The tree makes its appearance on the quilt—twisted and tortured as if in the throes of a strange agony, yet providing shelter for the broken bird.

The professors at the college are quick to notice Rama's intellectual superiority, her command of the written language, her original ideas, her versatile viewpoints. Professor Ramachandran, who teaches her English, is particularly intrigued by Rama's enigmatic style of writing. He watches her often, sitting by herself under the fig tree, and wonders what goes on inside her head. His suspicion that this has to do with some traumatic experience she had as a child is confirmed when, one day, he finds the usually quiet Rama berating a boy much younger than herself as she clutches a little kitten to her chest. The boy, who has found the stray kitten and has been poking it with a stick, is taken completely unawares by the ferocity of the tirade. He makes no attempt to defend himself as Rama, her eyes brimming with tears, tells him how unjust it is for strong, privileged people to victimize the weak, the frail, those who cannot defend themselves. The professor is quite taken aback at the scene, and decides the only way to help Rama is to reach out to her is through his daughter Parvathi, who studies with her.

Rama too, perhaps unconsciously, is beginning to tire of her self-imposed isolation. Initially, Rama is quite wary of Parvathi. In many ways, Parvathi is her very antithesis: gregarious and lighthearted, she has many friends. But there is a sensitive, thoughtful side to her that appeals to Rama. The two girls begin to share their lunch every day under the shade of the fig tree, and slowly the barriers begin to fall. The exchange of confidences is still limited though and, after a certain point, both recede into their own private worlds.

As they share more time together, Rama notices that Parvathi never visits Rama's home or the homes of any of their other friends, neither does she ever invite them over. She always meets them outside and goes home at a fixed time. After much persuasion Rama gets her home one day to meet her parents and Parvathi is overwhelmed by the welcome she receives from Shobha and Narayan. Pathetically pleased that their lonely daughter has a friend, they fall all over themselves to make Parvathi feel at home. Shobha has cooked pakoris and samosas especially for her and Parvathi is delighted with all the attention. But exactly at 6.30 p.m., the driver sounds the horn and Parvathi hurries to the door. When Shobha pleads with her to stay a little longer Parvathi gives her a quick hug and leaves, her face averted.

That night the squares on the quilt carry a version of the Cinderella theme: *A strong and confident bird, a blue one, has teamed up with the lame bird under the fig tree. But the blue bird always has to fly home at a certain time. Her sparkling blue wings are magical, but they have power only for a while. After that, they shrivel up and turn black.*

As Rama's motivation is rejuvenated, the old sparkle, the indefinable touch of brilliance, returns. Professor Ramachandran assures Rama that she will top the degree examination if she works hard enough. Rama forgets everything else, puts away her quilt, and plunges herself into her studies. She tries to infuse some of her own enthusiasm into Parvathi, who is strangely apathetic. Rama wonders why she is this way when she has such an erudite father. However, she tries her best to keep Parvathi interested and encouraged, and despite Parvathi's innate resistance her grades begin to improve.

One day, as Rama and Parvathi are heading towards the fig tree during their lunch break, someone comes up behind them and asks hesitantly, 'May I join you for lunch?' Rama and Parvathi turn around and exchange a glance of surprise for it is Renu, one of the most popular girls in the college, a part of the group that is always at the forefront of all the cultural activities in college. Renu delights the two girls with her company. She makes them laugh, talks with infectious enthusiasm about books they've never heard of. She also succeeds in drawing both Rama and Parvathi into the literary society and the dramatics society, and college for Rama becomes exactly as it was meant to be.

A green bird with a bright red beak and a white ring round her throat flies up to the fig tree. She is confident and unafraid. When the ugly creatures attempt to emerge from their cave, she attacks them and forces them to retreat into the darkness. The lame bird's wings begin to heal. She can actually fly now, although for short distances. The three little birds sit on the fig tree and chatter constantly. Sometimes they fly together, but they always return to their tree.

Renu gradually includes Rama and Parvathi in her wide circle of friends and welcomes them wholeheartedly into her family as well. Renu's father is a senior official in faraway Delhi and she lives in a large bungalow in an exclusive locality in Poona with her two uncles, their wives and their four children. Visiting her house is a delight for the girls. Her cousin brothers, Naresh and Umesh, are boisterous and always up to some mischief or the other; the girls, somewhat younger, are devoted to Renu and follow her around like puppies. Parvathi has a flair for painting and she is delighted to find that Renu's aunt is a talented painter and has a studio of her own to which she gladly invites Parvathi. Rama becomes an immediate favourite with Renu's elder uncle, a lawyer, who enjoys discussing his cases with her and is very impressed by her astute questions.

Just before the college closes for the autumn break, the literary society organizes a seminar on Romanticism. The topic of discussion is the influence of Romantic thought not only on European literature and culture, but on our own culture as well. Professors and scholars from other universities are invited to share their thoughts. The chairperson for the seminar is the famous exponent of the Chhayawadi movement in Hindi poetry, Madhavi Verma. A philosophy wrung from her painful and eventful life finds expression in her exquisite poetry. Renu has prepared abstracts of Madhavi's poems in English and distributed them to all the participants and students in advance. The imagery in her poetry is drawn from nature, everyday life and human relationships, but the theme is the oneness of human beings and god.

The seminar is a roaring success. The girls find Professor Ramachandran's paper particularly interesting for he sees the movement from a postcolonial point of view. His contention is that the Romantic Movement was not about love but about pain; it was born out of conflict and its greatest figures are tragic. There is no victor, only victims.

The green bird and the lame bird twitter excitedly, unravelling the implications of their new and marvellous find. The blue bird is still, and then she flutters her wings irritably . . .

Parvathi suddenly bursts out, 'You know, of course, that my father's paper was justifying himself to me!'

Seeing her friends visibly mystified, she continues, 'He's trying to tell me to forgive and forget. He insists that he is as much a victim as I imagine myself to be. Renu knows! My mother died six years ago. Her sister— she's a widow—came to live with us. To take care of me, they said!'

Renu interjects, 'But I've met her, and she seems quite pleasant.'

Rama continues to look bewildered, while Parvathi is only more furious.

'Yes, very pleasant indeed. Till she got my father to marry her and tried to become my mother.'

'Look, I know you took that very hard, and you haven't ever let us go to your house after that,' Renu says, her voice rising in exasperation.

'But . . . your father . . . how could he . . .' Rama breaks in.

'Exactly, and I'll never forgive him. He can talk of "victims" till he's blue in the face.'

Renu says mildly, 'But surely you remember all the ugly talk going around town; what else could he have done?'

Parvathi turns to her angrily, 'It's easy for you to talk! You have the most wonderful family. If you were in my shoes . . .' She stifles a sob.

'If I were in your shoes, I'd fight alongside my father and stepmother, not against them. You, my dear, are trying to make a tragedy out of a little tin-pot domestic incident! Grow up, Parvathi. You're not the centre of the universe!'

Rama concurs with Renu. 'You can't unmarry your parents, Parvathi. Besides, think of those who don't have a mother. Why don't you give your parents and yourself a chance?'

This is followed by more tears from Parvathi and more advice from her friends, but when she goes home that evening the burden sits lighter on her heart.

Thus, many more squares are added to the quilt— *the green bird and the lame bird are helping the blue bird keep the colour of her wings and, soon, they no longer shrivel up and turn black. In the process, the lame bird's wings are strengthened even further. Now she needs less of the green bird's help to fight the creatures from the cave.*

Soon after this, Renu's aunt, who lives in a nearby city, falls seriously ill and the family decides to visit her for a week. The large house will be left to the three older cousins and the servant, Shambhu, who has been with the family for three generations. Renu asks Rama to spend the week with her and, one evening, Naresh and Umesh, Renu and Rama find themselves seated at a dining table with a marble top that can comfortably seat sixteen people. Naresh, at twenty-three, is training in his father's profession—a trifle reluctantly, for, as a serious-minded intellectual, he would have preferred to build his career in the university. He has a wonderful sense of humour and his subtle witticisms keep the girls giggling throughout dinner. Rakesh is also full of mischief and Rama is forced to emerge from her shell and participate in the conversation. After the meal, when the girls are preparing for bed, Rama tells Renu that she has not laughed so much in her life. Renu looks at her quizzically and asks, 'Why?'

Flustered by the question, Rama stammers, 'Well, we too lived in a joint family once . . . but there wasn't much laughter in the house.'

Seeing her friend's obvious discomfiture, Renu changes the subject casually, 'You know what my father's favourite dictum is? "Laugh and the world laughs with you, weep and you weep alone, for the sad old earth must borrow her mirth, she has trouble enough of her own".'

It is summer and the nights being just barely cooler than the days the cousins decide to sleep out on the lawn. Always eager to fulfil the children's whims, Shambhu quickly lays out four camp beds complete with bedding and mosquito nets. Rama asks timidly whether it would not be better if she and Renu slept indoors. At this the irrepressible Umesh lets out a loud guffaw and says, 'Are you afraid of the big bad wolf? Don't worry, I'll protect you from all predators.'

Rama has become so unused to people being protective about her that tears of gratitude sting her eyes at this innocent statement and she jumps into bed to hide her tears. They talk and laugh late into the night, and Rama feels that she is being healed in some inexplicable way.

On the fifth night, there is a hint of a storm in the air. Summer storms, as violent as they are short-lived, are very common in these parts, and the beds are shifted under the covered courtyard at the back of the house. Late that evening the four of them settle themselves into their beds and have just started a game of bridge when the storms begins. The cold breeze drives sheets of rain across the lawn and the four youngsters whoop in joy as a light spray of cool, refreshing rain water brushes over them. Within fifteen minutes the storm has passed, but the four of them continue to sit in silence watching the raindrops glisten on the blades of glass as the clouds slowly move on and the sky clears.

By the time they go to bed it is well past midnight and the moon is high in the sky. The courtyard is paved in brick and has a tiled awning. It is open on all sides and surrounded by trees that cast grotesque shadows making Rama uneasy, wishing she were back in the safety of the house. The others are almost asleep and Rama climbs into bed and draws up a sheet to cover herself. An owl is hooting somewhere and its call is answered by other sleepy birds. A mouse scurries across the brickwork and into the rustling, dry leaves. The heavy scent of the blooming jasmine permeates the air as she drops off to sleep.

An hour later, Rama awakens, shivering. A light breeze has come up. She sits up sleepily and is just about to draw a thicker sheet over herself when she catches sight of a strange figure covered in white from head to toe but obviously female inching towards them from the end of the courtyard. Rama's heart leaps into her mouth, her blood turns cold and an incoherent yammering flows from her lips in a continuous stream. The next to awaken is Umesh. He sits up and is frightened out of his wits when he spots the figure approaching them. In one bound, he reaches Rama's bed, slips under the net and puts his arms around her. Rama, terrified of physical contact of any sort, is amazed to find that a broad male chest and strong arms can actually provide comfort and clings to him. Then Renu awakes. She shakes Naresh so violently that he almost jumps out of bed, startled. The least imaginative of the lot, and the most sensible, he calls out loudly, 'Who's there?'

The figure stops for a moment, but starts moving towards them again. Naresh calls out for the darwan, but the gate is too far away for his voice to be heard. Fortunately, the servants' quarters are just beyond the courtyard and Shambhu comes running with his son, Rameshwar. Without the least hesitation, he goes up to the white-clad figure and demands, 'Who are you? What are you doing here at this unearthly hour?'

Silence! Shambhu asks again, more roughly this time. Slowly, the figure lifts the pallu covering from its face and reveals a very human, though very terrified face. Rameshwar's eyes light up as he recognizes the woman. He suppresses a smile and whispers something in Shambhu's ear. The change in Shambhu's expression is dramatic. He asks her a few questions and speaks to her reassuringly, then steps back deferentially and tells Rameshwar to take her into their quarters. The four young people who have been watching this charade with bated breath, now attack Shambhu with questions. Rather shyly, Shambhu tells them that the lady is

Rameshwar's mother-in-law. Apparently, she was supposed to pay them a visit but had lost her way from the station and arrived late. Renu and Naresh now turn to Umesh and Rama, who are still clinging to each other, and burst out laughing. Drawing the dwindling shreds of dignity about him, Umesh claims that he had only been comforting Rama, and she vociferously agrees.

The incident has a cathartic effect on Rama. The next evening, her last evening with them, she tells Renu the story of her early life in all its traumatic detail. Renu listens with sympathetic and avid attention. As she reaches the end of her story, Rama breaks down completely and Renu holds her friend close till she is able to compose herself. Rama is amazed to find that Renu is neither horrified nor repelled. Instead, she says in a matter-of-fact tone, 'You think you are alone in your suffering, but my uncle can tell you stories of incest and child abuse within families that will appall you. In any case, who has emerged as the victim? You or your cousins? They are doomed to a life of perversion, while you have every chance of making a success of your life if you fight hard enough. And you've already proved to yourself and everyone else that you can!'

That night Rama goes home and works on the quilt till dawn.

The lame bird and the blue bird sit on a thorny bush trying to get nectar out of the icy blue flowers. They are, however, frustrated in their efforts by the sharp prickles which prevent them from getting to the nectar. The green and red snakes slither around the bush looking to slake their own thirst. The thorns prick them too and draw blood. The birds are delighted at their discomfiture, but distressed about their own failure to reach the nectar. Weak and parched with thirst, they begin to shed tears that form a little pool. Another stream made from the tears that the snakes are shedding finds its way into the pool. Then the green bird alights on the bush. She looks around, hops closer to the other birds, and points to the snakes. She flutters her wings and a magical transformation takes place—the birds and snakes take on each other's forms. Yet, they are no closer to the nectar and the thorns are as sharp as ever. Then the green bird attacks the thorns, and the snakes and the other birds follow suit. Bloody and lacerated, they continue to strive till suddenly the thorns turn into flowers, icy blue and full of nectar. After all of them drink to their heart's content, they gather around the pool of tears and look at their reflections. There are no shakes now, neither are there birds; all they can see is a medley of colour.

1984

Birthmark

TODAY THEY TRIED TO DESTROY A SHRINE THAT HAS STOOD FOR over two hundred years near a crossroads in the older part of the city where I live.

It is a friendly little edifice with four minarets, a dome, crazy china flooring and a tiled plinth. A bird had dropped a seed into a cranny about a hundred years ago and a banyan tree had grown into the very walls and foundation of the structure, so you could not destroy one without damaging the other. A few of the locals had got together and built a paved platform around the bole of the tree that projected beyond the mosque, and a shivalinga had been placed on it within a temple-like niche. During Shivaratri, the festival of the god Shiva in February, women in brightly coloured saris brought their offerings to the deity in burnished brass and copper thalis: five different fruits, flowers (the purple and white akand, essential for the worship of the great god, and the datura), leaves from a bel tree, fresh milk and holy water from the Ganga. They repeated the pujari's chants after him, then placed their offerings before the idol and bathed it with milk and the holy water. Some of this mixture flowed through a channel at the base of the linga into a large brass bowl and was consumed by the women as charanamrit, the nectar flowing from the feet of the god, to break their twenty-four-hour fast. Then they collected the prasad and went home like a flock of bright birds chattering about the day's deed well done. The unmarried girls prayed for the perfect husband; those who had daughters prayed for the birth of a son; those who were childless prayed to be rid of the curse of infertility. The older women prayed for the welfare of their households, and the widows for an early release from a life of misery. The deity—dark and inscrutable—listened to all their pleas but seemed to pay scant attention to these insects who thought they were the ones who turned the wheel of life.

I live in a house across the road. I stand at the window often and watch the constant activity around the shrines. It is a source of perennial interest to me, as much as it helps to while away many an idle hour. The call for namaz goes out at the appointed times. Five times a day, regular as clockwork, men don their caps, bring out their prayer mats, face Kabah and lose themselves in their prayers. Very often prayers are offered simultaneously in both sanctums. In fact, I have even seen some young people surreptitiously nudge their neighbours to say a prayer on their behalf to the other deity!

I did not always live here, though. My family lived in the affluent, more cosmopolitan part of the city. Our neighbour, Mr Khan, was a family friend and his daughter, Kulsum, my constant companion from earliest childhood. We played in each other's spacious gardens, shared the same swing, exchanged toys and ate off the same plate. Kulsum's mother was a fabulous cook, as was mine. And between the biryani and kebabs and alu paratha, puris and raita, we had the best of both worlds. We went through school together and then, at my father's insistence, Mr Khan sent Kulsum to college, although her mother was in favour of an early marriage. In her second year in college, Kulsum met a young man, very intelligent and polished, who was training to be a lawyer. As their friendship deepened, however, a tragic truth came to light—a rare, incurable disease was drying out the optic nerves in both of Asif's eyes and he had only a few years' vision left. One evening, Kulsum came over to my place to spend the night. Neither of us slept a wink. Like two squirrels in a cage, we endlessly debated right and wrong, love and sacrifice, success and failure, money and poverty, duty and freedom. A pair of innocents bred in ivory towers debating on the mysteries of life with total conviction in their arguments and analyses; the gods of our respective creeds must have been amused.

In the end, idealism won the day and I held Kulsum's hand as she broke the news to her parents one evening. They were naturally dismayed and did their best to dissuade her, but to little avail. Finally, they agreed to meet Asif and were immediately captivated by his charm and sincerity. The marriage was a quiet one, in keeping with the wishes of the young people. Kulsum became not only Asif's wife, but his secretary and, later, his legal assistant. She did all his reading and writing, made summaries, prepared points and briefs, and read aloud to Asif till he had a clear picture. Then he brought his exceptional powers of logic and imagination to bear on the facts. The combination of their talents created courtroom drama that took legal circles by storm. Within ten years, Asif had lost his eyesight but was the most sought-after criminal lawyer in the city. They had two children, Laila and Iqbal. For Kulsum, the day she met Asif was the most blessed day in her life. So far, idealism had paid off. Or so we thought.

I came to this house thirty-five years ago as a bride. I was twenty. I had to wait to complete the first degree at the university because my father had insisted that I get an education, hence the late marriage. My mother-in-law had been very concerned that her only daughter-in-law was not only 'old' but educated as well, and might not fit too well into the pattern of the joint family system.

When the marriage had been arranged relatives had whispered that it was a rather unusual match. My in-laws were neither as well known nor as well off as family. Why, they had wondered, had my parents found me a middle-class home with its attendant problems? Was it because I was dark and did not meet the standards of a market that valued only fair brides? Was my father merely trying to save money? Could it be that he wanted to retain his 'superior' position vis-à-vis his son-in-law?

One day, my cousin's father-in-law, Mr Vyas, paid us a visit. He was the patriarch of a family that outshone us all, our friends and every relative, in wealth and prestige. His family exemplified generations of material success, traditional values and conservatism. Our family could never have aspired for an alliance with his but, in the manner of a fairy tale, he had seen my cousin Rohini at a college function where he was the chief guest. He had been captivated by her stunning good looks and demanded her hand for his second son. My uncle, aunt and the rest of the family had been overwhelmed by this stroke of good fortune and had fallen all over themselves to comply with his wishes. My father and my grandmother had tried their best to point out the inequality of the match but their warnings were ignored. The marriage had been solemnized five years ago. Rohini hardly ever visited us. She was too busy holidaying abroad and hobnobbing with the rich and famous. When she did come, we noticed that she smiled a lot less than she used to.

Mr Vyas had made an appointment. Precisely at 5.30 p.m., his chauffeur-driven Rolls Royce purred up the driveway and stopped under our portico. He had particularly expressed a wish to meet my grandparents and parents and naturally they were a little apprehensive of the purpose of the visit. He refused all the refreshments except a glass of fresh lime juice and, without much ado, came to the point.

'I believe you have arranged Krishna's marriage.'

'Yes ... we have ... a very eligible boy,' said my grandfather.

'What does he do for a living?'

'Dinesh is a chartered accountant and works in a good company.'

'His monthly salary?'

'At present about Rs 2500, but he has prospects ...'

Mr Vyas's eyebrows steadily climbed up his spacious forehead.

'And on that salary he expects to support a wife?'

'Well ...'

'His family is well to do, no doubt?'

Realizing my grandfather's discomfiture, my grandmother spoke up. 'As a matter of fact, theirs is a joint family. They are comfortably off, but not rich.'

'Do they have a home?'

'Yes.'

'Where?'

'In ...'

Mr Vyas' eyebrows disappeared into his receding hairline and he began to splutter. 'But ... but ... that's a terrible locality! So middle-class!'

My father, who had been listening with an amused expression, now cut in smoothly. 'Absolutely! Lower middleclass, I would say!'

'You expect Krishna to live there?'

'Yes. We also believe she will be very happy there.'

'How?'

'Well, they are an educated and close-knit family. Krishna will get a lot of love, I'm sure.'

'Does the boy own a car?'

'No. It will be a long time before he can buy one—secondhand, of course. But I'm training Krishna to use public transport.'

Mr Vyas could only shrug his shoulders in dismay. When he left, he told us condescendingly that he would come to the wedding but it would not be possible for him to attend the modest reception Dinesh's family was planning. True to his word, he came to the wedding and gave me the heaviest piece of gold jewellery in my entire trousseau. Rohini did not come. She dropped by for five minutes on the morning before the wedding, looked at Dinesh's photograph for a long time, gave me a quick hug and left.

Years later, when Rohini, still childless, had lost her good looks and had practically become a recluse, we discovered that her husband had always preferred the company of his own sex. His father had picked Rohini in the hope that her looks would wean him away from his predilection. My father lost no time in bringing her away. He arranged the divorce and insisted that she pick up the threads of her life afresh; we were all there for her.

On the issue of my marriage, my father had tackled the innumerable questions with his usual aplomb. He insisted that his son-in-law, a self-made man, would value his daughter more than a spoilt young man from a well-to-do home. He was certain, too, that I would adjust to my new environment and not let him or myself down. Even so, the whispers continued till the last day. My mother, quite at her wits' end, had suggested breaking off the match but my father was adamant.

'Do you want your daughter to be loved and respected or do you want her to be treated like some commodity? Let her live, let her struggle. Why should she spend her life like an ornament on a shelf in a drawing room? That's not how we brought her up.'

Why had he been so insistent? Why this obsessive preoccupation with people 'valuing' his daughter? In the dim recesses of my memory, in the remotest corner of my heart, I knew there was an answer, that my father had very good reasons for his decision, but at that time I was not entirely sure. However, I did not question him at any stage and, after the usual fanfare of the wedding, had come to live in this modest house, which my father-in-law and his brother had built.

My husband was the eldest in the family and since I was his wife everybody in his home had their expectations of me. I had come fully prepared to make adjustments, curb my needs, and become a part of the family. My grandmother had told me that since love can tame wild beasts, it should be perfectly possible to placate my in-laws with genuine affection and tact. In the beginning, all went well. My father-in-law and his brother liked me to serve their morning tea and insisted that I bring my cup along. I read the newspapers to them and we had lively discussions on politics, the Upanishads, the novels of Premchand, the film industry, and human iniquity in general. There was an interesting collection of potted plants on the terrace and they entrusted these to my care, for they knew I missed the spacious and beautiful garden in my father's house. After this morning session I moved into the kitchen to work with my mother- and aunt-in-law. They were relieved to find me fairly docile and adept at housework and quickly initiated me into the household preferences. I joined them in my mother-in-law's room after lunch and read aloud from the *Ramayana* or the *Mahabharata* the portion they had marked out for the day, while they listened and nodded off intermittently.

However, there were days when life seemed hard, when the daily grind of domesticity seemed meaningless, when a longing for freedom ached in my soul and threatened to overwhelm me. Early spring was the worst time of all. The gusty winds shook the trees and blew away the old leaves in swirls of dun, russet and gold. For a few days the bare branches called out to the skies with uplifted arms in seeming supplication. Then, miraculously, the sap ran strong and the new leaves burgeoned and grew and engulfed the brown in a million verdurous shades. The birds, quiet through the long winter, mated furiously and built nests with single-minded devotion. Most of them would be blown away by the strong winds, but it didn't seem to matter to the birds; they merely picked up the wisps and began again. The festival of Baisakhi marked the official advent of summer. Almost on cue, the brilliant flame-of-the-forest, the flaming gulmohar, came into flower, and the narrowest alley in the city was transformed by a riot of colours and fragrance. I thought of my father's garden where the misty violet jacaranda and the canary-gold Indian laburnum flowered in unison at this time of the year, creating a synthesis that was almost painful in its perfection. And, of course, the cuckoo, hiding in the flowering mango trees with their dense foliage, sang its heart out for anyone who cared to listen. And I did; the poignant call permeated my entire being and filled my soul with a longing that could not be denied. Longing for what? Perhaps for an alternative destiny that had been within my grasp, almost, but had somehow eluded me?

I did not know. At such times I would retreat to my terrace garden and fight and struggle——for acceptance, for courage and for faith in life——till I was exhausted. Was it not the tenet on which I had been raised?

My husband had struggled hard to acquire an education, as money had been scarce when he was growing up. He had worked part-time as a bookkeeper in the evenings to pay his tuition fees. At the end of the tunnel, a good job had been waiting for him, and he had risen quite quickly to a respectable position in his firm. His marriage to me had helped his self-esteem and I could see that the chip on his shoulder was slowly but steadily diminishing in size. I encouraged him to accept people as they were, to be less critical, to believe that not everyone in the world is driven by an ulterior motive. It was not easy; he had been hurt and deceived too often. But he was learning to trust and his faith in himself and in life was gradually resurfacing. I prayed that he would have time to let it strengthen, become durable, so that when the next blow came he would be able to bear it better.

My husband's cousins, Ramesh and Rakesh, were so different from each other that anyone who met them would certainly begin to believe in the myth of changelings! They were much younger than my husband and thus, had not had to struggle so hard. The family had paid for their education. Ramesh, who was an engineer, was a trainee in a government undertaking; Rakesh had not trained professionally. He had dropped out of college halfway through and gone into 'business' with his friends. No one in the family was quite sure what his line of work was, for even when he was at home, which was rare, he mostly kept to his room. He had plenty of money and made a solid contribution to the household expenses. Nobody asked him where the money came from, and if they did Rakesh had just one answer: 'I give my share, don't I? How does it matter how I do it?'

He was the only one who had not been happy when Dinesh had got married to me. On my wedding night, he had told me, 'You are obviously a golden bird in a golden cage. How will you like living in an iron cage with a bunch of crows?'

His eyes, dark, unsmiling, piercing, had bored into mine for a moment, and then he had turned away. After that he had hardly spoken to me and I too left him alone.

My father, I think, was well aware of my struggle. He seemed to have anticipated it and prepared for it in his own unique way. Right from the beginning he created strong ties between the two families with a constant exchange of ideas and an abundance of activities that could be shared, like picnics and family holidays. The gifts he sent were never for me or Dinesh alone, but for the whole family—books, music, magazine subscriptions and a parrot that the whole family loved and everyone tried to educate after their own fashion! Without anybody really noticing, barriers continued to fall and the intimacy increased, till a solid bond held the two families together based on mutual respect and trust. It was most important for me that my parents and family members had won the love of my in-laws and had, in turn, come to appreciate the latter's sterling qualities. This took the strain out of the adjustments I inevitably made and allowed me to settle down at my own pace.

Rakesh was the only member of the family who noticed these subtle changes. He was displeased about them and frequently vented his irritation in barbed comments. One day, at teatime, when Dinesh's aunt was proudly doling out pieces of a cake she had baked using one of my mother's recipes, Rakesh looked her squarely in the eye and said, 'So, you too have fallen under the spell of the golden bird and are beginning to pick up the vilayati ways of her family.'

Noticing that his mother was at a loss for words, my mother-in-law smoothly interposed, 'We are merely saving money by baking a cake instead of buying one. I have never noticed an aversion to cake in you before this evening!'

A gale of laughter greeted this remark, but Rakesh was not easily outdone. Baking a cake, he said, was to actively participate in a non-Hindu activity. For, in India cakes are made by Christians and Muslims and such insidious influences would slowly weaken our traditional culture and pave the way for alien influences. No one took much notice of him that evening. Maybe we should have.

Unlike my family who had lived in this town for the last four generations, my in-laws had been citizens of East Pakistan who were compelled to flee India when the partition came about. This was the main reason for their reduced economic status. In spite of all the hardships they had had to face, I found them remarkably free of resentment and parochialism. My mother-in-law would often say, 'The suffering has not been ours alone. What of the miseries of the other side? In any case, we created the conflict ourselves and walked into the trap with our eyes open. So who are we to complain?'

My father-in-law still had business contacts and friends across the border with whom he exchanged letters quite frequently. Their visits were rare, but joyous occasions. My in-laws' relationship with their neighbours, many of whom were Muslims, was amicable. Very often, Mrs Mirza, who lived next door, would accompany the ladies of our house to the mosque-cum-temple. There, they would part, say their prayers, meet again and return home together. When I asked my mother-in-law if I could invite Kulsum home one day, no eyebrows were raised and my friend was welcomed with open arms. So charmed were they by her that they would remind me to call Kulsum when I forgot!

Five years passed. Dinesh was rising steadily in his profession and worked longer hours. I had a little daughter, Shravani, who kept me very busy. I also had to shoulder greater responsibility in the household as my in-laws grew older, but I always found time to tend to my plants and to spend fifteen minutes at my window which faced the crossing and the shrines. The constant flow of people, the steady faith that drove them, the variety of personalities, colours and emotions fascinated me and comforted me in a strange way, as though this was the one certainty in my world of shifting sands.

Meanwhile, the elders were thinking of finding Ramesh a bride. The usual rounds of proposals, talking to relations and friends about suitable brides, was in progress. My aunt-in-law suggested a cousin of mine who was a frequent visitor to the house and whom everybody liked. Ramesh too was not averse to the idea, but Rakesh disagreed. The family did not want another educated daughter-in-law who would spend time with books and plants, he said. Ramesh should marry into a conservative, influential family and establish connections that would benefit them in the future. His friend's sister, Rajni, was perfect for Ramesh; she had all that a good Hindu family required—she was pretty, young, malleable and very devout. Ramesh was not very keen. He said feebly that she would not get along with his friends, but Rakesh insisted that she did not need to. If she pleased him and his family, that should be enough.

That very evening, Rajni's brother, Rajnish, came with the formal proposal. Three servants followed him with sweets, mewa and presents for the family on silver salvers that they put down modestly on the floor. When my mother-in-law protested, Rajnish said politely that in their family this was the custom. One did not visit future in-laws empty-handed. Surely, the same rites had been followed when Dineshbhai was married? After the formal discussion was over, I brought in sweets and sherbet on a tray and put it down before Rajnish. He immediately got up, folded his hands and said, 'Bhabhiji, my sister is not as well-educated or as accomplished as you are. Will you please train her to your satisfaction?'

There was a veiled mockery in his eyes that belied his words, a look that I was to encounter again and again under varied circumstances. When Rajnish was leaving, my mother-in-law asked if she should have the salvers placed in his car. Rajnish smiled and said, 'Maa-ji, in our culture we never take back anything from a daughter's new house except blessings.'

He then touched the elders' feet with great reverence, bid polite adieus to Dinesh and Ramesh, looked meaningfully at Rakesh and left.

Although the visit produced mixed reactions, Rakesh painted such a rosy picture of Rajni's family's affluence and influence that the elders had little to object to. Dinesh could not say too much for obvious reasons and kept his misgivings to himself. Within a month, the formalities had been completed. After a lavish wedding that was a nine-day wonder in our town, Rajni came to live with us.

Shravani, now six, was ready for school and Dinesh had decided to admit her to the missionary English-medium school where I had been educated. My in-laws agreed as the school had a good reputation and the teaching staff was very competent. This decision, however, evoked a stormy protest from Rakesh, who felt that the liberal education dished out by these schools was at variance with the traditional culture of our home. Shravani should go to a girls' school that was run by a religious trust and where the language of instruction was Hindi. Since Rajni's father was one of the trustees of this school, Shravani would be welcomed with open arms. He was sure he had won the battle of wills, as usual, when my mother-in-law, rather unexpectedly, said, 'I think Dinesh should have the final say in his daughter's affairs. Shravani is clever. She deserves a good education.'

This remark, of course, played straight into Rakesh's court, and the debate that ensued went to the heart of the cultural divide within our family that was yet in its nascent stage. One view was that all humans are born friends, and enemies are created only for a purpose, so one should guard against making enemies and resolve all conflicts peacefully. The other view was that men are born friends and enemies. To strengthen the friends' hand and oppose the enemy with every ruse, strength and stratagem available was man's moral duty. It seemed to me then that our living room was a modern Kurukshetra, the famous battlefield of the *Mahabharata*. Morality, that great double-edged sword, was out of the scabbard. Who would wield it, finally?

This round went to Dinesh. Shravani went to my school. She also began to spend more time with my family as the school was near my father's house. However, she remained very close to her paternal grandparents and they took care of her homework and leisure. When the school invited me to take up a job in the primary section, Dinesh supported me and spoke to his parents. They were equally supportive for they realized that Rajni, in her quiet but determined way, was taking over the reins of the household and that I was being steadily marginalized. If I spent the better part of the day away from home, the possibility of conflict would be minimized. I joined school and soon found myself immersed in the simple joys and sorrows of the young children. The time I spent with them rejuvenated me and kept me distracted from the petty troubles that I knew would be waiting for me when I got home everyday.

When Rajni bore a son within a year of her marriage, her position as the 'Lakshmi' of the house was ensured. She had fulfilled a need that I had failed to satisfy, and was now the custodian of our family's future. The family name and tradition would be perpetuated through her progeny. Rajni's father presented his grandson with a cheque of one lakh rupees and a fifty ounce gold chain when he saw him for the first time. We were all suitably awed and failed to realize that this was an opening gambit in a takeover bid.

After this, Rakesh got married, and Sonali, Rajni's cousin, also brought a huge dowry with her. The house that we had lived in for so long was not luxurious enough any more. The neighbouring property, belonging to a Muslim family, was acquired at a throwaway price. The modest house was razed to the ground and a mansion, gleaming with glass and marble, came up in its place. We had assumed that we would all move to the new house as a family, but Dinesh proved unexpectedly obstinate. He had a lot of affection for the house his father and uncle had built with their hearts' blood. His boyhood and youth had been spent in it and he wanted his daughter to grow up here and treat this as her home. This gave my father-in-law the opening he needed and he too decided to stay on. Strangely enough, our uncle and aunt also wanted to stay back, but Ramesh and Rakesh would not hear of it. Ultimately, they agreed to move with great reluctance and with the rider that they would return if they found the new house difficult to adjust to.

The house-warming ceremony was to be a lavish affair. Everybody who was anybody was invited. But when my mother-in-law said, 'We must send cards to the Khans and Kulsum and Asif' she came up against stark silence. Finally, very gently, Rajni explained that her family would not like 'non-believers' to be invited to the puja that would consecrate the house. We could call them over some time later, perhaps. Dinesh and I did our best to pour oil on troubled waters, but my father-in-law and his brother were adamant: they would attend the puja minus their friends, but would not spend three nights in the new house as per custom and would return immediately after the ceremony. Finally, Ramesh and Rakesh did send the cards, but the invitations were politely refused as our friends were 'otherwise engaged'. The ceremonies were performed. All the men and women of the family circled the house three times and then entered it together. The festivities continued for a week but, true to their word, the elders returned home, and the breach was never healed.

The next few years were hard. Between Dinesh's salary and mine, and my in-laws' pensions, we managed to make do, though very modestly. Rakesh and Ramesh constantly offered to help, but we were loath to accept anything from them. While we struggled along, counting our pennies, the house next door flourished like the proverbial green bay tree. A son was born to Rakesh and once again the town was rocked by festivities. And there were, of course, all the religious festivals that were celebrated with increasing pomp, grandeur and charity. Poor people were fed on all occasions and the term 'annadata', giver of food, was used frequently by the local poor while referring to the two brothers. Slowly, Rakesh and Ramesh were emerging as the local leaders with a strong Hindu following.

The years were blurring by. Laila and Iqbal, Kulsum and Asif's children, and Shravani, all attended the same school and were doing well. Close to graduation, they were beginning to think of career choices and, increasingly, the option of studying abroad seemed preferable. In our youth, the Mecca had been England; now it was the US, with its wonderful universities and generous scholarships to attract promising aspirants. The lack of opportunities in the home country, the necessity of the 'right connections' to get on in life, provided further impetus. My in-laws were initially a little concerned about letting Shravani launch out on her own but she was their only grandchild and they would never stand in the way of her dreams. My parents were very keen that Shravani should make good use of the opportunities I never got. Dinesh and I bowed to the inevitable. We had noticed, as had Kulsum and Asif, the growing closeness between Shravani and Iqbal. While we were delighted about the relationship, we realized the stormy passage it would have in our hometown. So the US it would have to be, for all three of them.

All three children were fortunate enough to gain admission into first-rate institutions, but even with scholarships there was quite a bit of financial shortfall. Asif, a flourishing professional, could just about manage. But Dinesh and myself, who had no savings, were at a loss. Even if we took loans and I sold my jewellery, it would not be enough. We began to avoid Shravani's anxious eyes. My in-laws even considered eating humble pie and asking Ramesh for a loan, but Dinesh would have none of it.

Then, one evening, my parents came over. Their visits were always happy occasions for they got on famously with my in-laws. After the usual rounds of tea and lively conversation, my father announced that he had learnt a new magic trick that he wanted to show us. Lights were duly dimmed and the windows shut. We sat in a circle holding hands while my father stood in the centre and chanted strange words. We did not know whether to laugh or take him seriously. Finally, he called Shravani out, made her stand before him, put his hands on her shoulders and inquired, 'What do you want most in the world, my child?'

No answer.

He asked again, in a more insistent tone, 'Tell me. If you don't, the magic won't work.'

And then, Shravani, her voice shaking, came out with her anguished heart's desire. She wanted, desperately, to go to the US with Laila and Iqbal, to build a career for herself so that we would all be proud of her. Her pathetic words lingered in the air and there wasn't an eye that was dry in the entire circle.

Then my father's voice rang out again, 'So be it, my child. Close your eyes and give me your hand.'

There was a rustling of paper and Shravani was suddenly looking down on cash certificates that would pay for her education abroad several times over! It seemed that my father had been investing steadily since her birth for just such a contingency, and his delight at being able to play Father Christmas was palpable.

After this came a continuous blur of activity. One fine evening, several sets of grandparents and two sets of parents stood in the lounge of the international airport, bidding goodbye. Ramesh and Rakesh and their families also came, full of misgiving about this radical course of action, but impressed with Shravani's achievement nonetheless.

That was almost fifteen years ago. Much water has flowed since under the bridge of time. The three children are settled in the US with good jobs. Shravani and Iqbal are married and have a child. Laila has married an American colleague and is happily bringing up a son. My parents and Dinesh's father and uncle passed away in quick succession. Now our house is occupied by the two old ladies, Dinesh and myself. Dinesh has retired, but has set up a consultancy that keeps him busy. I still work at the school. My mother- and aunt-in-law run the household. In the evenings we sit on the terrace garden and speak more and more of the past, as the present becomes less and less intelligible to all of us.

A few days ago, Asif and Kulsum paid us a visit. They were very disturbed. For some time now, clients have been avoiding Asif and brief after brief has been withdrawn. They have discovered that several Muslim professionals, including doctors, are in the same situation. There seems to be a concerted drive, though very subtle, to smirch reputations, cast aspersions, raise doubts about their work. The city has recently been rocked by a scandal involving a well-known Muslim physician and a woman who claimed he had molested her. Other stray incidents have been equally worrying. Fires have broken out in quite a few bustees, but the people who have lost their hutments were always Muslim. My little mosque increasingly wears a deserted look and though the call to namaz is announced five times a day, it is a whisper of its former self. The temple, on the other hand, is gaining popularity by the day and it enjoys the patronage of the great house next door more than ever before.

Things come to such a pass that Kulsum and Asif decide to emigrate to the Middle East much against their will. The town that has been home to them and their forefathers has suddenly turned into a jungle where fear stalks them constantly. Saudi Arabia with its fundamentalist regime will be anathema to them, but they have no choice. Nor are they the only ones. Several other families have also decided to leave the country. Kulsum and Asif have dinner with us the night before they leave. My mother-in-law and my aunt break down completely when the time comes to bid them goodbye. They cling to Kulsum as though she is the last vestige of the world they knew.

The next evening when Dinesh and I return with heavy hearts after seeing off Asif and Kulsum we find the lights on in the sitting room and the two old ladies sitting with tearful faces with Ramesh and Rakesh, who are looking very ominous indeed. They have come to warn us that riots are imminent in the city and that widespread violence is to be expected. We may be targeted because we have Muslim friends and have committed the sin of allowing our daughter to marry a Muslim. They suggest that we should move into their house, at least for a few days. Dinesh refuses to be intimidated. The brothers then insist that their mother and aunt should go, but neither is prepared to leave us. Finally, Rakesh blurts out angrily that none of this would have happened if it had not been for me. My friendship with Kulsum, my encouragement of Shravani in her waywardness, my entire attitude, always at variance with good Hindu norms, is unacceptable to the powers that be. He says that we have escaped so far because we are related to Ramesh and him. Once the riots begin and the mob takes over, they may not be able to help us at all.

Dinesh is seriously concerned and tells me to take indefinite leave from school and stay at home. He warns the servants about possible intruders and tells them that for a few days they will have to run all our errands for us and ensure we don't step out of the house.

That night I lie awake and think of many things—my parents, Shravani, my childhood, my garden, my in-laws, Kulsum, Dinesh—but most of all, I think about the woman who appears from time to time in the locality and sets up home under a wayside bauhinia tree for a few days. Clad in rags, filthy from head to toe, her hair matted and orange, she sits in the lotus pose under the tree, her eyes closed. The sunlight, filtering through the shiny green leaves and bright pink flowers, falls on her body, on her face, on one breast exposed through the rags. That she was once beautiful is apparent, for the grime can neither hide her lustrous skin nor her fine bone formation. In front of her are two vessels in which people pour water and leave food. She never makes any attempt to 'get' anything for herself. One day, as I was passing I saw her urinate in her water pot and drink the liquid to quench her thirst and wash her face. Totally outraged, I asked her, 'Why did you do that? Are you not ashamed to behave like this?'

With a faint smile on her lips, she opened her eyes for a minute and said, 'Shame? What is shame? Do you not know that all is one?'

Then she closed her eyes firmly, and for the rest of her sojourn under the tree I could not get another word out of her despite my best efforts. Tonight, I think of her words again and again and wonder … Life, I realize, is like a piece of tapestry; an embroidered picture of perfection that exists only in our imagination. Reality is the obverse side of this picture, full of knots, tangles, crossed threads and confusion. There are no norms, principles or values that are absolute—only the status quo. Each individual, each generation must define and endlessly redefine what is 'right', for it is a word so glibly and carelessly used that it has lost meaning. The naked struggle for material power that uses religion as a façade is as old as religion itself, yet it must be played out again and again, only with different actors and on a different stage. What can people like us, weak and ineffectual, do in such a situation? How can we get through to the sane this mad woman's message: All is one?

Confined to the house, I have more time to think, to feel. It is as though every pore in my skin has become more receptive and I can soak in the tension, the hatred, the avarice that permeates the air. What irks me most is my own cowardice and inactivity. Surely I can take some action, speak out? I don't have to concentrate totally on self-preservation. But Dinesh's worried face and my in-laws' helplessness hold me back. Day melts into night and dusk into morning.

Increasingly, I think of an envelope that lies behind my clothes in my steel cupboard. It was given to me by my father a few days before he passed away. He had said, 'Perhaps you will never need to open this, for it contains information that you can well do without. However, if you ever face a dilemma, moral or otherwise, and feel the need to communicate with me, then do take a look at the contents.'

Today I think of his unbending principles and realize that the hour has come. I must hear his voice again.

Late at night, when the others have fallen asleep at last, I light a candle and with the envelope in hand head for a corner of my terrace garden. I place the candlestand on a ledge, sit down on the floor and open the envelope with trembling fingers. Inside are two sheets of paper covered on both sides with writing in my father's strong hand. The paper seems to carry the scent of his cigar. Suddenly, he is very close ... I feel he will lay his hand on my head at any moment. Uncontrollable tears blind me for a few moments. Finally, the words stop dancing and blurring on the paper and I am able to decipher them.

> Dearest Krishna,
> We called you that—your mother and I—because your glossy, dark skin, near-perfect face and mass of shiny black hair made any other name impossible. In any case, the name you told us was yours when you came to us—Munni—was not a name we could keep calling you by ...

A cold hand clutches at my heart, my head swims ... When I come to, I find myself lying face down on the floor, the letter lying under my furiously beating heart. I get up, splash some water on my face, take a hold on myself and start reading again.

> The time has come, Krishna, to tell you a little story.
> You remember how you loved the stories I made up for you as a child about the demons and fairies that lived at the back of the garden? This story though your mother and I wrote only partially, for fate wrote the beginning.
> As you know, Krishna, your mother and I were very happy together. When we got married people said we had both been born with golden spoons in our mouths. Health, money, education, good

humour, we seemed to have it all. The first five years of our married life were ecstatic, and it took us a while to recognize the growing need within both of us for a child of our own. We had been visiting doctors for some time when we came to realize that maybe this was one blessing that God had denied us. Your grandmother was very concerned and kept begging us to go to Salim Chisti's dargah in Fatehpur Sikri to pray for a child. Legend says that a son was born to Emperor Akbar after he visited the great Pir and was blessed by him at Fatehpur. It was to commemorate this event that he built the amazing palace there and tried to make it his capital instead of Delhi. It was the desire to please my mother, more than anything else, that took us to Fatehpur.

The dargah at Fatehpur is an amazing place. You have to complete the rituals, then tie a thread on its latticed walls and pray for a child. If your prayer is answered, you go back with the child to show your gratitude. You will remember, I'm sure, the trip we made with you when you were ten years old?

I remember only too well. It had been a most enjoyable trip. We had visited Delhi, Agra and then wound up at Fatehpur. I can still remember my awe at my first view of the Buland Darwaza and my father's voice telling me

how this great palace had been built as a second capital
and then abandoned for lack of water.

Your mother and I, educated sceptics, found
ourselves in a strange frame of mind on that day.
Science had informed us that we could not have a
child. What were we doing here? We had originally
thought of visiting the dargah but not taking part
in the rituals. But once we joined the people
proceeding to the darga, we were pulled along in
spite of ourselves. When we were told that we
must tie the thread together as man and wife, we
found ourselves strangely moved; your mother
actually had tears in her eyes.

However, once we were away from the palace,
rationality reasserted itself and we looked rather
sheepishly at each other. We also decided to visit
the palace before returning to the guest house.

On the dark terrace, all alone, surrounded by plants,
the fragile flame of the candle flickering in the breeze
and casting eerie shadows, the occasional splash of a fish
in the pool—the only sound apart from my own
breathing—I feel strangely disoriented. Who was I, then?
Who had been my real parents? Was my entire identity
borrowed? A fear I cannot control takes possession of me
and I shake as though with high fever. But when I put my

hands to my face I find it is icy cold. I don't know how long I remain sitting in this state. Ultimately, I force myself to return to the letter.

> At the palace we were compelled to join a group of visitors and listen to the guide who was taking us on a tour and making up history as he went along. After about fifteen minutes, we had had enough and began to lag behind. So busy was the guide with the intimate details of Akbar's life that he did not notice us slipping away. We found a quiet courtyard, mercifully empty, where sunlight filtered through the stonework and the shrubs that were growing in the crannies, and sat down on a convenient ledge to rest our legs. Neither of us had understood the strange emotion that had gripped us in the shrine and, though we had been puzzling over it in our minds ever since, we still did not know how to discuss it with each other. Finally, your mother blurted out, 'Do you think what we experienced at the shrine had anything to do with faith? Or were we just swept away by the local colour and atmosphere?"
>
> Her voice was deliberately casual straining to hide a pleading note of hope. For once, I, the conscious intellectual, had no answer. So I just put my arm around her and, cheek to cheek, we

stared at the sunlit courtyard where the shadows were beginning to lengthen. And then, as though by magic, a toddler, just over a year old tottered out from behind a bush and came straight towards us. Yes, Krishna, that was our first encounter with you. Mesmerized, we watched you cross the width of the courtyard. Then you put your little hand on my arm and said, 'Bhukh!'——you were hungry. When I asked, 'Tumhara naam kya hai?', you answered, 'Munni.' Your mother had some biscuits in her bag, which you ate with great concentration. Then you held up your arms and said, 'Godi'. When I took you on my lap, you leaned your head against my chest and went to sleep.

Believe me, Krishna, we did our best to find your parents. We asked everybody in sight and made inquiries with the police. Finally, after three days, the local OC told us to leave our address with him, so that he could get in touch with us if your parents turned up. But he never did.

We returned home with you. Strangely, you did not cry at all, but behaved as though you had known us all your life. Perhaps you had, in another place, at another time ... Who knows?

I try to cast my mind back to some memory that pre-dates my parents. But there is nothing before their total love.

I was on the point of taking up an assignment outside India at that time and, because we wished everybody to think you were our child, we expedited our departure. I explained to your grandparents that your mother was expecting a child and that I did not think it was good for her to travel too much. They were so overjoyed that they consented to let me take her along, and within two weeks we left with you for Bangkok. But you know about that. You remember your friends and the school there with so much affection.

He is right, of course. But the only thing I remember now with great nostalgia are the brilliant cascading orchids in every home, store and street corner.

When we returned three years later, everybody was so charmed by you that no questions were asked. In any case, I had taken care to build up a strong web of circumstantial evidence, with photographs, mementoes, toys, that was totally convincing. Besides, your grandmother took the entire credit: had she not sent us to Fatehpur to the dargah? I wonder whether she ever realized how right she had been.

We have no idea to this day how or why you came to us and we did not want to know. For you were God's greatest gift to us. Krishna, Draupadi of the *Mahabharata*, after whom we named you, had a tumultuous passage through life. She was aided at every stage by her friend, Lord Krishna. The Lord himself came from Devaki's womb, but was raised by Yashodhara and Nanda, his foster parents, with total devotion. I think the analogy is clear. Love has no parentage, colour or creed. It is life's greatest and least understood gift. I want you to remember this when you are in doubt. There is no force that is equal to or can combat love.

Dearest Krishna, if the soul is eternal, if there is another life, if we ever meet again, we three, then your mother and I have no greater wish than to have you as our child again. How you came or come to us is immaterial ... for, more than flesh and bone, it is the oneness of spirit that is immutable. Fire cannot burn it, water cannot drown it, the wind cannot sway it and time has no power over it. Love transcends life, time, space; it came out of Pandora's box holding its foster-child by the hand—mother and daughter, love and hope.

Your loving father

My tears have been falling for some time, but the feeling that I will never see him and my mother again in this life is now so acute that I begin to weep uncontrollably, the letter clutched to my heart ...

At last, the paroxysm subsides and I try to regain control of myself, when suddenly, out of the blue, the mad woman's words come to my mind: *Do you not know that all is one?* Like fireworks going off and revealing fleetingly the secrets of a dark night, I too experience a momentary illumination. My parents have not gone away; they are very close to me tonight. I can feel their benediction upon my being. Only, I lack the wisdom to lift the veil and reach out.

Exhausted with the travails of the night, I drop off to sleep. The next memory I have of that night can be nothing but a dream. Lots of people, many colours, varied sounds, a babble of voices. I am there, but there is no image of myself, I am moving of my own volition, but not aimlessly. Something or somebody seems to be carrying me. The power that is guiding me has a definite aim, a purpose. A little while later, I am lowered to the ground but I cannot move. I cannot breathe. And then it comes—a piercing pain as something hot and sharp jabs into my chin, three times. The pain is unbearable. I scream, again and again. I am still screaming when I wake up drenched with sweat. The sky is beginning to lighten in the east, and I am still sitting in the garden. The candle has gone out a long time ago. The birds are beginning to stir. My body is so stiff that it is difficult to get up, but I do. I go down to my room quietly. Mercifully, Dinesh is still asleep. I put away the letter and go in for my bath. My mother-in-law will soon need my help to start the puja.

On this day, when I need to be alone to sort out my thoughts, I am caught up in an endless round of household duties. Our relatives next door have invited themselves over and our usual spread is too bland for their palate. Between shopping, cooking and cleaning, the day flashes by and I am just arranging a few flowers in a vase, when the doorbell rings. The guests are here. Rajni and Sonali have both put on weight and, in their expensive clothes and jewellery, are walking exhibitions of their husbands' prosperity. The boys, both still in school, would come to this house much more often if they had their way, but are kept on a tight leash by their parents. They now sit between the two grandmothers and demand stories.

'Stories? What kind?' asks my aunt-in-law.

'Of your childhood, of course. And about our fathers. You keep saying the world was so different then. Tell us how. Tell us about Shravanididi. Was she naughty as a child?'

Shravani is not mentioned much by this part of the family since she married Iqbal. Now Rakesh, who still wears his lean and hungry look, admonishes them.

'Stop pestering your grandmothers. Why don't you go and watch TV?'

Since this is what they do every evening of their lives, the boys are not at all keen to move. Ultimately, the two grandmothers go into the next room with them. The sound of lively conversation and laughter filters through to ours, making Rakesh distinctly uncomfortable.

After dinner, which the boys enjoy thoroughly and Ramesh too tucks into heartily, we sit together in the living room. Ramesh leans back and blurts out, 'It's good to have home-cooked food once in a while. Our cook is good but he's very careless.'

He turns to his mother, 'Can we send him over for some training?'

His mother smiles and says, 'Your aunt and I gave up the kitchen a long time ago. You will have to ask your bhabhi. She cooked everything you ate today.'

Ramesh, caught on the wrong foot and aware of Rajni's eyes boring into him, quickly tries to recover lost ground.

'Bhabhi was always a good cook and now she's become an expert. Of course, she cooks regularly and that is the secret. You don't have a cook, do you, bhaiya?'

This last question is directed at Dinesh, who answers curtly that he cannot afford one. The silence that follows is deafening, and Rakesh charges into it with all his force.

'We've come to warn you for the last time. The trouble could begin tomorrow. Please do not show your faces or say the wrong things. I'm telling you again, if you do anything wrong, we will not be able to help you.'

I have not slept much last night and not had an iota of rest during the day. My nerves are perhaps on edge and, suddenly, I cannot take this smugness, this self-assured knowledge of 'right' and 'wrong', any longer. I turn to Rakesh and ask, 'What makes you so sure that you have a monopoly on what's right? No one is born into a creed, people are merely initiated. Is your own blood completely untainted? Is mine? How much do you know of your ancestry? Or of all the women who have come into this house as wives? Careful, Rakesh. I too am warning you. Take care that the ground that you think is so firm beneath your feet does not give way under you.'

Tears are threatening to overwhelm me and I leave the room. Very soon after, I hear subdued voices on the doorstep. Then the voices retreat, the door is closed and very quietly everybody retires to their rooms. Dinesh goes into his study. I know he is giving me space and I am grateful.

I am exhausted, but I cannot sleep. My eyes burn as I stare into the darkness, trying to come to terms with everything that has happened in the last twenty-four hours. I realize that the knowledge that I am adopted has not upset me at all; it has only increased my respect for my parents and strengthened the bond if possible. It has also endorsed my belief that love depends neither on circumstance nor on social constructions, and as I now know, not even on blood-ties. This knowledge has liberated me. No, what is worrying me is the strange dream I had. In an odd way, I feel that the dream provoked my uncharacteristic outburst tonight. Where does the connection lie? Is the dream a memory from my infancy? I have encountered nothing in my conscious life remotely like it. The questions swirl like endlessly spinning balls on a roulette board till I feel my head will burst. Finally, I rise, splash some water on my face and stand before the mirror. Does my face hold a clue to the mystery of my identity?

I am dark but I have clear skin and even now I don't have too many wrinkles. I lean forward and scrutinize my face closely. Arched eyebrows, large, limpid eyes, aquiline nose, slightly full lips, a firmly rounded chin, and on my chin a birthmark, just where a beauty spot is usually painted. My grandmother used to say with great affection that God had placed a mole on the face of Tilottama, the perfect woman in mythology, for he had not trusted man to do it right. Now I look closely at this birthmark, run my fingers over it gently. For the first time I realize that it is not a regular mole, for the skin is not raised at all. No, it is not a birthmark, but just a mark. I recall again the searing pain in my dream, and at that moment everything falls into place.

This is no birthmark, but a tattoo to indicate my heritage. In north India, only girls from Muslim and lower-caste families are permitted to tattoo their skin.

Upper-caste families consider it shameful. I have an insane desire to laugh, to go and tell Rakesh the truth just to see his expression. In the end, of course, I do nothing; for too many people who love me will be affected. I fall off to sleep though, with the words of the mad woman who sits under the bauhinia tree ringing in my ears. *Do you not know that all is one?*

The trouble begins three days later. A slum, with tenements constructed mainly of bamboo, straw and polythene, is torched in the dead of night. It turns into an inferno within moments. The residents escape with their lives, but their meagre possessions turn to ashes before their eyes. There is no source of water close by and the police and the fire tenders turn up only when the whole area has been reduced to a heap of smouldering embers. This slum is mainly occupied by Hindus and the cause is taken up by the powerful contingent that controls the city. One of its most vocal members is Rakesh. He puts the blame squarely on Muslim neighbours who, he proclaims, have done this to enable more Muslims to settle in the vacated area. These theories are debated with great vigour in the newspapers and soon become the only topics of conversation in the city. Friends and neighbours of long-standing suddenly look askance at each other and the trust that has been built over the years collapses like a house of cards. The little mosque is practically deserted now and the Hindu devotees too are fewer in number. People keep to their homes, terrified of what the morrow will bring.

One afternoon, Mrs Mirza comes over with her daughter-in-law, who is about my age and with whom I have a good relationship. The elders exchange reminiscences over cups of tea, while Nazli and I mainly listen and speak only when their failing memories require support. The memories are happy ones and it is good to see them so animated and relaxed. Finally Mrs Mirza comes to the point. She is afraid, for her house is adjacent to the great mansion next door and lately Rakesh and Ramesh have been ignoring her family completely. A little wicket gate in the boundary wall that gave access to the Mirza compound has been covered with barbed wire. Her sons too are taking precautions, arming themselves, but they do not want the conflict to spill over into this house. What she wants to know is, in case of trouble, whose side will we take?

Silence hangs heavy in the air till my aunt, realizing it is actually her decision more than anybody else's in the family, turns to any mother-in-law and asks, 'Tell me, Didi, what should I do?'

The question echoes like the chimes of a bell and we all wonder how much courage we would have had in her situation. But my mother-in-law is not daunted. She says, 'You will do what you think is right. Do you not see you are facing—no, all of us are facing—the same predicament that Arjun did on the battlefield? It is a question of deciding between two loves—the greater and the lesser. However, this is not your choice alone, but ours too, and Mrs Mirza's and Nazli's. They too must give their word to choose wisely.'

In a tearful voice, my aunt-in-law counters this argument.

'But what was the outcome of Arjun's choice? Total devastation, complete annihilation. Not a child was left alive, not a soul to weep for them when they went on their last journey. How do we know what the right choice is? And if we do, can we live with the consequences?'

The air, like the stretched string of a bow, is taut with uncertainty. Then my mother-in-law smiles and says, 'Don't worry, Chhoti, we will not repeat the mistake they made at Kurukshetra.'

Nazli blurts out, 'What mistake, Mausiji?'

'They left the decision-making to the men, Nazli, instead of to the people most concerned. Do you think the battle would have taken place if Kunti and Gandhari, the mothers, wives and daughters, had taken to the battlefield? If they had stood between the two armies, would the arrows have flown? We are all mothers here. Today we will make a pact not only to oppose wrong, but also to do what we think is right. After that, we will go to all the women in this locality and ask them to join us. Then we shall see who is stronger.'

So, on that evening, when the sun is going down in all its glory and the birds are returning to their nests, the five of us swear that we will act in unison when the time comes, for the future is ours to mould and create.

The next few days are spent in indefatigable campaigning and suddenly I find that my burden is lighter. It was for this day that fate had lifted me from my place of birth and brought me here. We are amazed to find how many of the neighbourhood women are prepared to join us, even the ones on the 'winning' side. They are afraid of the future that their husbands and brothers are about to create, afraid that their children will have to pay in some way. So the net widens and very soon we have with us almost five hundred women of varying ages prepared to fight, to take affirmative action. I find that my mother-in-law is right, as usual. Mothers have no creed except motherhood. We have in our sorority not only Muslims and Hindus, but Christians, Sikhs and Jains. We realize that religion is not the dividing factor; greed and avarice are. And a victim is a victim irrespective of belief or faith.

The next chapter opens with conflict over a pond about a mile from our house and deep within a sprawling slum. As it is the only source of water in the area and is used for bathing and washing clothes and utensils, the local inhabitants take great care of it. It is kept completely clear of garbage, grass grows on its verges and the trees on its edges provide shade and shelter. One side of it is paved and has steps going down into the water. These are called ghats and are mainly used by women because the trees that line these pavements offer them some privacy. It also serves as the local community centre. In the evenings, children, parents and grandparents assemble there to exchange news, discuss current affairs, philosophize.

Since this is a mixed community, areas are clearly demarcated for Muslims and Hindus. The wiser people realize the absurdity of trying to put dividing lines in water, but go with the majority to avoid conflict. Bamboo palings have been placed across the middle and a rope with coloured floats tied to it stretches between the stakes. Children sometimes forget and venture to the 'other' side, but are always called back by vigilant elders. This line, though, disappears in the evenings, when the two communities mingle freely and the only symbols that differentiate the mothers of the two sides are the burkhas and the saris.

It is out of this closeness that the trouble springs. One fine morning, Saif, a young labourer in a nearby factory, is found to be missing as is Rampyari, the eighteen-year-old pretty daughter of Bhairon, who works in the same factory. Intense search on both sides fails to reveal a single clue. Ugly rumours begin to circulate as people start discussing how they could have eloped so secretly. Frustration mounts within both communities and threatens to escalate into violence. The people who have orchestrated this move by finding a job for Saif in a faraway town and giving the couple a large sum of money are just beginning to congratulate themselves when the news arrives at our house via Nazli whose maid lives in this area that Saif's mother has taken to her bed for she knows that he will be lynched if he is ever found. If not, her younger sons, Alam and Amir, will not be spared.

My mother-in-law wastes no time. She summons as many members of our network as she can at such short notice. That evening, about two hundred and fifty women of all communities seat themselves on the grass next to the pond and request a meeting with the spokesmen of both communities. The men are taken completely by surprise and make an appearance looking distinctly apprehensive. They have never encountered so many determined women, together, in their lives.

It soon becomes clear that the men have no personal feelings about the matter; they are expressing an outrage they do not really feel merely to discharge their duties. Next, we request the presence of the parents—Bhairon and Maya, Asad and Sabbo. On being closely questioned, they admit that they have nothing against each other's children. If their religions had not been different the marriage would have been celebrated with great joy. Abruptly, Asad asks whether Bhairon will agree to conversion if the couple ever return. Bhairon reacts in the negative with an aggression he is obviously simulating. Maya, looking fearfully at her husband, says, 'I would not mind. My religion is not as important to me as my child's happiness or life.'

Encouraged, Sabbo speaks up, 'I too would be happy to accept Pyari if she converted.'

Mrs Mirza now asks a simple question, 'Will you be able to change Pyari's face, her limbs, her body, her nature?'

The men look at her as though she's gone mad. Undaunted, she continues, 'Obviously not. But you can compel her to change her religion. Tell me, how valuable is something that can be changed so easily? Look at this pond. All your lives depend upon it. You have placed a marker, but have you been able to change the water? Even if you build a wall to separate the two sides, would you be able to control the rain that feeds it?'

Her questions linger in the air and it is evident that they have made an impact. Suddenly, Nazli's maid, who is with us, directs a question at her mukhia.

'What about the boy you found at the fair three years ago and brought home because his parents could not be traced? You have been raising him as your own son ever since. Did you bother to find out whether he was Hindu? No, you took him to the mosque and informed the authorities that he was your son and you wanted him to be raised as a devout Muslim. If you had children of your own, would you have reacted differently?'

Before the embarrassed mukhia can find a reply, Maya presses home the advantage.

'What would you do, mukhiaji, if he grew up, realized he was Hindu and disowned you?'

By this time, a sizeable crowd has gathered and issues of birth, parenthood, religion and love are being hotly debated. Before we leave, Mrs Mirza and my mother-in-law have extracted a promise from the women that they will not allow anyone to take action without due deliberation. Whatever the decision, it will be born out of dialogue not impulse.

Matters seem to settle down over the next week or so. Out meetings are held regularly and some local newspapers write appreciatively about our efforts and initiative. One evening, we return from a meeting to find Dinesh sitting alone in a dark room. He looks so haggard and pale that we think he must be ill, but he merely hands me a filthy piece of paper with crude writing on both sides. We are Muslim-lovers. We have given a daughter to a Muslim and so violated every decent Hindu sentiment. Dinesh and I are using the elders as shields, taking advantage of their simplicity, but the people 'in the know' are not deceived, nor will they tolerate further 'immorality'. This is the final warning. The language in the note is execrable and abusive. The paper has been wrapped around a stone and thrown through a window. Dinesh found it lying among the shattered glass when he returned half an hour ago. I have never seen Dinesh so shaken in my life and we realize his predicament. He feels responsible for our security, but we are making it impossible for him to protect us. My aunt walks up to Dinesh, lays a hand on his shoulder and says gently, 'Don't worry, my son. We will maintain a low profile for the next few days and see how things go.'

Three days later, at about two in the morning, I awaken to the sound of metal striking stone, brick and mortar at regular intervals. For a moment, recognition eludes me ... then I identify the sounds for what they are: the rhythmic blows of sledgehammers and crowbars methodically destroying an edifice. I had fallen asleep over a book, so the lamp is still on. I switch it off and rush to my window. Men wrapped in dark sheets with blackened faces to avoid being identified are standing around holding flaming torches while others are methodically, deliberately, destroying the little mosque ... my mosque. By the time Dinesh and I come downstairs, my mother- and aunt-in-law are already waiting by the door, their faces dark with anxiety. It is a *tableau vivant* that I will not forget as long as I live. Their faces, lined and furrowed with age but beautiful and strong as ever, caught between pleading and caution, between two loves, craving absolution; Dinesh, facing the greatest crisis of his life, looking helplessly at me; and I, with secret knowledge of my origins in my heart, the realization dawning in me that the debt I owe to life must either be paid tonight or remain forever unrequited. Then my mother-in-law takes her sister by the hand. Dinesh and I follow like two docile children, and together we step out of the house into the night.

By the time we are close to the mosque, however, the blows are fewer in number and some sort of confusion seems to be prevailing. The miscreants have broken down one wall and a door and have damaged one of the minarets of the mosque. But to get to the inner sanctum that houses the Koran, they have to break down a wall that is firmly held in place by a particularly thick and tortuous root of the banyan tree. Branches of the same root have lodged themselves in the temple and to destroy the root the temple must be broken and desecrated first. The miscreants are now discussing, in urgent whispers, whether setting fire to the tree might help. But this idea is quickly abandoned, for the banyan itself has semi-sacred status among Hindus; besides, it is huge and strong and will not burn easily.

As we strain our ears to try and keep track of the hushed conversation, we turn around to find members of our club, with Mrs Mirza and Nazli in the vanguard, marching steadily towards us. Without a word, Mrs Mirza walks up to my aunt and mothers-in-law and takes their hands in hers. Nazli, Dinesh and I follow suit and, as the other women join in, the cordon begins to lengthen.

It snaked its way
Inch by inch,
This living chain
Of mortal links,
Past the blackened
Men with bars,
Who had been told
To 'do' not 'think'.
One swung his bar
With measured force,
And watched the old,
Weak woman sink.
But the breach
Was filled by one
Whose hair was whiter
Than the last.
She smiled at him
And bowed her head,
Waiting for
The second blast.
Now unconscious
Of caste or creed,
They knew they had
To do or die;
For the living
God within, they
Could not, would not

Ever deny.
So the chain held
Steady and strong,
Though many fell
From time to time;
Till the mighty men
Turned tail and fled,
Far, so far from
The scene of crime.

Dawn is breaking and the birds are beginning to stir, when Dinesh and the other neighbours call an ambulance for the injured women. Ramesh and Rakesh emerge at last, presumably to inspect the extent of the damage, and find their mother injured and writhing in pain. They rush to her side to help her. She raises her head from the ground and looks into their eyes and says, 'Beta, see how god takes care of his own kingdom when his children fail him? What can you or I or anyone do against His will?' Ramesh and Rakesh follow my mother-in-law and me back to our house, supporting their mother between them. After she has been put to bed, I brew some tea. Dinesh returns and, as everyone settles down with their cups, I tell my family the greatest secret of my life. Ramesh and Rakesh, clearly horrified, are wondering whether to spit out the tea they have swallowed unwittingly. Dinesh and his mother just smile at me and at each other.

It seems they have known all along. My father had hidden nothing from them. They had welcomed me into their lives with full knowledge, affection and trust.

Dinesh and I are the 'elders' now. When I look back on my life I only have one regret: that I have never again met the woman who sat under the bauhinia tree, though I look for her every day. Perhaps I will see her one day, when the time comes, when the past meets the present and the future and all becomes one ...

Afterword

NONDA CHATTERJEE WAS BORN IN 1938 IN CALCUTTA. HER personal life, like that of the city, was a dichotomous one in which she traversed the two equally arbitrary realities of colonial existence—the native culture and the one imposed by British rule.

As the author herself says of the stories in this collection, 'These voices have been in my head for a while and these stories were waiting to be told. This is my attempt to preserve the memory of the many extraordinary women I have met during the course of my life.' True to her commitment to her characters, Chatterjee has seemingly absented herself from the telling. But her technique is so compelling that the events in the stories unfold in a natural sequence, and the authorial voice seems to provide only the necessary background on the complex class and caste configurations of feudal India. As is apparent from the tales, British rule seemed to have negligible effect on the realities of the lives of women in India regardless of whether they were from poor families like Heeriya in 'Motherhood', or the daughters of the educated and well-to-do Professor Mukerji of 'The Rose Garden'. Very few women received adequate schooling and, for the great majority, life remained confined to the circle of marriage, reproduction and finding a precarious toehold in their husbands' household. The British showed little interest in fostering rapid social change in India, and were content with the economic benefits and the geopolitical stature that the possession of overseas colonies entailed.

Indian nationalists for their part, even the more liberal-minded members of the elite, viewed the family and women as sacred sites of national culture that were to be guarded from the onslaught of the imperialists. While the early part of the nineteenth century was dominated by the efforts of Indian social reformers to deal with horrible social practices such as the prevention of widow remarriage, widow burning, child marriage and polygamy, once the nationalist movement got under way at the end of the nineteenth century, these issues were buried under the anti-imperialist rhetoric. Women's liberation was dealt a serious blow by the new xenophobia that sought to protect an imaginary national culture at any cost. Attempts to prevent child marriage or to universalize female education were often criticized as capitulation to the senseless demands of westernization. As a result, while individual and exceptional women achieved success and independence as doctors, lawyers, politicians and educators, there was little in the way of an organized feminist movement in India until the 1970s. Chatterjee's heroines do not expect social support or even gender solidarity. They struggle mostly alone, without resignation or bitterness, but with an everyday heroism and selflessness that seems extraordinary in our times. Their expectations are modest, and when they do receive kindness from a stranger they view it as an unexpected gift.

The stories are not tied together by the theme of social reform or the lack of it, but by a shared world view, a belief that an underlying unity pervades all reality. A deeply Hindu concept, the notion of oneness is the antithesis of the binary oppositions that structure Western thought and life. A non-Westerner who reads St Augustine's *City of God*, will be amazed at the polarized thinking that pervades the text—one has a clear choice between the City of God and the City of Man, and nothing lies in between but the dark chasm of confusion and hell. Hinduism on the other hand is a lot like life— messy, difficult to decipher and composed of overlapping concepts and symbols that defy categorization, and sometimes, even comprehension. Thus to a true Hindu there is no life and no death as both these states are equally illusory and equally transient. Heeriya's death at the end of 'Motherhood' cannot be called a tragedy, as there is little to separate her bodily existence from the one that is yet to come. Similarly the sacred and the profane are in a continuum and one leads inexorably to the other. To the Hindu mind the carnal and spiritual are inextricably linked and the erotic relationship of the gods and goddesses have inspired a most lyrical and spiritual cycle of myths and legends. For Rama, the protagonist of 'The Quilt', it is physical passion that destroys her childhood and yet it is her own emergent sensuality that reanimates her interest in life.

Even one's identity, the inalienability of which provides the bedrock of all Western thought, is represented as a slow-moving target where the ascriptions of gender, class, religion, caste rarely find their mark. Krishna, the protagonist of 'Birthmark', is initially repelled by the beggar who her own urine and washes herself with it but, as the story progresses, events peel away the various layers of artificial identity that have coalesced to create her sense of self. In the end we are left unsure about Krishna's real identity, is she a Hindu, a Muslim, a dutiful daughter-in-law, a rebel community activist? Is there nothing to separate water from urine?

The second theme that pervades these stories is one of empowerment and self-help, both buzzwords of contemporary Western feminism. Chatterjee, however, presents a version of Indian feminism of her generation, one that is imbued with notions of duty to the family and community. Western feminism is based on the underlying autonomy of the female subject and seeks to endow her with a voice, authority and an inviolate wholeness. Chatterjee's heroines are less whole both in the corporeal and the spiritual sense. While the image of the raped and battered female body occurs repeatedly in her prose, the act of violation is represented in non-sensationalist prose and sometimes as an almost inevitable rite of passage. Rape often functions as a metaphor for sex in the deeply feudal Indian society and sometimes as a complicit act in which a woman uses the institution of rape to further her own ends. Thus Dulari, in 'The Trial', discovers the higher meaning of gratitude and love in the sordid act of seduction and rape. For Dulari there is no love without sacrifice and she realizes that it is necessary to sacrifice the body to further the spiritual ends of her soul. She repays her debt and helps the cause of Indian nationalism, but even the most degrading act cannot defile a soul when one's intentions are pure and one's motives are selfless.

Few of Chatterjee's heroines are self-aggrandizing, or even ambitious. They survive, improvise, manufacture meals out of potato peels, bury husbands, rear families and raise children. When they are roused to action, it is always in the interests of the family and the larger community. While Chatterjee writes about Indian feudal society with a fine eye to historical detail and an unemotional acknowledgement of the terrible conditions that Indian women live in, it is greed and selfishness that rouses her ire. Her villains are beyond redemption and Chatterjee rarely pauses to analyse the motives for their malice. She accepts the existence of evil as an unfortunate but quotidian phenomenon, as something that women have to grapple with on a daily basis. Ultimately it is a combination of luck, tenacity and a simple desire to make the most of the hand that life has dealt that sees these women through. They rarely have the luxury of choice, of flight, of remorse or regrets, and it is not pure happenstance that Chatterjee's favourite maxim holds that only those who have the courage to endure life will survive.

Choi Chatterjee

Glossary

Agrahayan	a month in the Bengali calendar which usually falls around 15 October and 15 November
babul	thorny tree with yellow flowers
bai	part-time maid
Basanta	festival of spring
besan	gram flour
beta	son
Bhabhiji	elder sister-in-law
bhojali	dagger
bhukh	hunger
Bou	bride
Chhoti	young one
Chini	sugar
chulha	coalfire
Didi	elder sister
elaichi chai	cardamom-flavoured tea
godi	lap
gulal	red powder dye
Jaagte raho	keep awake
Janamashtami	festival celebrating the birth of Lord Krishna
jowar, bajra	millets
Kabir, Rahim	religious poets
kulin	one belonging to any of the families on whom an order of honour was confirmed by King Ballal Sen of ancient Bengal

Lakshmi puja	worship of the goddess of wealth
lehnga–choli	long skirt and short top
Maa-ji	mother
madol	a medium-sized cylindrical drum played on by tribes like the Santhals
Mai-Baap	mother and father
matras	vowels
Mausiji	aunt
mewa	dry fruits
mukhiya	headman
nagraj	king of snakes
namakharam	traitor
neelkanta	Durant
pakoris, samosas	tea-time snacks
pichkari	spray pump
raag-prodhan	a semi-classical composition
rajdoot	royal ambassador
Ram Ram babuji	God be with you, sir
Ramcharitmanas	Tulsidas's version of *Ramayana*
Ranima	queen mother
Shivalinga	phallic idol made of stone
Shona	gold
sindur	red powder applied along the parting in the hair or on the forehead as a dot as a symbol of marriage
surkhi	powdered brick